So Far from Home

The Diary of Mary Driscoll, an Irish Mill Girl

BY BARRY DENENBERG

Scholastic Inc. New York

Skibbereen

County Cork, Ireland

1847

Thursday, April 1, 1847
Skibbereen, County Cork, Ireland

'Tis true.

I will be going to America.

I can remember when I first heard the name. AMERICA.

Visiting Aunt Nora, we were, just Ma and me. As far back as I could remember Kate and Da stayed behind. Ma would be baking morning and night, while Da smoked his pipe as if 'twas his last bowl. I could always smell a visit coming.

Before we left I'd work on my lessons. Aunt Nora was teaching me English. Ma was proud that Aunt Nora was a teacher and could read and write. Ma wished she could, too, I think.

To be sure, Aunt Nora was always glad to see us, she having no children of her own, only the children she taught.

I was eight the last time we visited. After that she left for America. 'Twas then I first heard the name.

Sitting on the beach, we were, watching the waves come in and breathing the fresh, salty ocean air. Aunt Nora loved the ocean.

"Come sit by me, Quiet One." She called me Quiet One because Kate, my older sister, was rarely still.

She motioned for me to come closer. I was thinking she was about to tell me a great secret. I scurried across the sand like a crab until I was as close as could be.

"Do you know where America is?" she whispered.

I didn't.

"Look out toward the horizon. What do you see?" she said.

"Only sea and sky," I answered. Try as I might 'tis all I saw.

"Can you see past the sea and the sky?" she asked.

I couldn't.

"There lies America," she said. "Past the Isle of the Blessed, where the mermaids bask on the rocks. Past the Land of the Lost, whose earthly forms cast no shadow."

I dared not move, charmed as I was by the sound of Aunt Nora's voice and the stories she told.

"Even past the Land of the Fallen Angels, where the seagull has no voice. There lies America. 'Tis a sacred place where everyone dresses in red, the color of magic, and the roads are paved with gold.

"'Tis in America that you'll live someday, Quiet One."

Then Aunt Nora fell silent, worn out, it seemed, by the thought of this faraway land, this America.

I told Ma as soon as we returned to Aunt Nora's cottage, so excited was I by this news. Ma smiled and put her arms around me — she smelled of spice and honey. "Your aunt is as sweet as a whistle but there are times when her speech is more crooked than a ram's horn. Pay it no mind, Mary dear."

Now Aunt Nora's letters from America are the only bright spot in our lives. Ma and Da sit silently while I read them aloud. She writes of the opportunities in America and urges us all to join her. America, she says, is the land of hope.

She has sent a ticket for my passage along with this last letter. I can't help but think back to that day by the sea. I was thinking Ma was right, that 'twas just Aunt Nora's way of talking, and I paid it no mind. I never dreamt it might someday come true.

Friday, April 2, 1847
Skibbereen, County Cork, Ireland

I will be leaving in three weeks. Ma said it this morning, and I have been like a cat on scissors ever since.

Da was not pleased, though I am not sure why. Maybe 'tis because the family is being further scattered about. Maybe because Ma had not told him of her decision. He gave no sign.

His silence made me uneasy — as it always does. Relieved, I was, when Ma began speaking.

"All the girls are parting. Kate has been there

two years, and Nora six. 'Tis Mary's time now. My sister will look after her."

Da stood up, his pipe gripped tightly in his teeth, and walked to the door. "Fine, fly away then. At once, across the sea to America. 'Tis all anyone cares to talk about anymore. America. A place where people have lost their senses. I wish you Godspeed, daughter."

When Da was gone, Ma turned to me. I have never seen her look that way.

"Mary, you are no longer a child. Praise God you are young and strong. Go to America — 'tis our only hope."

Ma is right. I am strong. Although I am only fourteen — three years younger than my sister Kate — I do not mind. I have always depended on Ma and Da. Now 'tis my turn. I won't let them down.

Maureen is the only one I told. We've never had any secrets. She would like to go with me, but her family has no money for the passage. She said she will be lonely when I'm gone. 'Tis sad. I miss her already.

Saturday, April 3, 1847
Skibbereen, County Cork, Ireland

'Tis best I go. We are down to nothing. Once
the potato provided us with all we needed. Now
we are always hungry. 'Twas two years ago — I will
never forget — when the fog came in and I heard
the dogs. They could smell the foul odor. 'Twas
warning us, they were, howling until the morning
light.

At first Da was thinking soot had fallen on the
potato crop. But the blackness spread to the dark
green leaves and the purple blossoms. The leaves
crumbled to ashes at his touch. When he dug
down into the ground he discovered only a slimy
mass of rotten potatoes. Fear in his eyes, there was.

Now there's not a loaf of bread in all Skibbereen. We line up for soup, but 'tis of poor qual-
ity and leaves us hungry just the same.

Our neighbors kill their animals to last another
day. We have sold our furniture so we could have
money for food.

Da talks of help coming from England, but Ma
says that is foolishness. The English care nothing

about the Irish. You can't get blood from a turnip, she says. I suspect she is right.

The roads are littered with lifeless souls wandering about. They look more like walking ghosts than flesh and blood. One funeral follows another. Fathers bury their daughters, wives their husbands — all without a tear being shed.

Now there is only an eerie silence. No cackling chickens disturb the morning silence. No dogs bark in the night — for they are either dead or too weak to cry out.

My hand is trembling as I write. I sleep little and wake often, soaked in a cold sweat.

The world is coming apart at the seams.

May God have mercy on our souls.

Wednesday, April 7, 1847
Skibbereen, County Cork, Ireland

Two more weeks. I thank Almighty God for Aunt Nora sending the money to bring me out. She is working hard in America, teaching her students, so I can come. I am fortunate to have such a generous aunt. She says the ticket is a gift from Kate as well, but I doubt if that's true. Kate is not one to share any of her wages with me. She has yet to send us money for food.

When I am settled in America, 'tis me who will be sending the money home so Ma and Da can join us.

Aunt Nora says there is a need for girls who wish to be maids-of-all-work in respectable homes — such as where Kate works. American girls do not care for that kind of work. 'Tis beneath them, she says.

Kate likes the work. She works for the wife of the mill agent, Mr. Abbott. Aunt Nora asks that I tell her if 'tis factory work I would be seeking. If 'tis she will talk to Kate. Aunt Nora is sure Mr. Abbott can help me find work in the mills.

Ma is relieved to know that Kate is getting on well, since we never hear from her.

Aunt Nora also asked that we write her what ship I will be on. She will be sure to meet me in Boston.

I would like to work in the mills. 'Tisn't for me

to be someone's servant, like Kate. A day's pay for a day's work, that's what I say.

Living in a rich lady's home is not for me. I don't like being at someone's beck and call. I'd rather know what my tasks are and then be left on my own. Even helping Ma with the chores I prefer it that way. When we still had the sheep I would do all the clipping. When Ma taught me to card and spin, I did it all on my own so Ma could tend to other things. The same with baking the bread and feeding the pigs. Lord knows, the work was never finished, but there was no one looking over my shoulder.

'Tis best I work in the mills. That will suit me. Aunt Nora writes that the pay is better in the mills, and the higher the wages, the faster we will all be together as a family.

Her letters make America sound filled with promise. 'Tis a place, she says, where a girl can work hard and be rewarded. 'Tis all I ask.

All around us the landlords are evicting people. The Dalys had their cottage tumbled down three days ago. 'Twas brought to the ground in the wink of an eye. A frightful scene there was. Mrs. Daly was racing about clinging to her doorpost — the only thing remaining of her home.

Ma fears we will be next. If Mr. Hughes takes our cottage from us, we will have to turn to the poorhouse for relief. Ma says she will never allow that. She says that those who go in do not come out alive.

I can hear her sobbing at night, although I dare not stir.

We will be happy in America, God willing. I can hear it in Aunt Nora's letters.

Ma says it's counting our blessings we should be. Unlike those around us we are not ill. The Sweeneys are suffering from the black fever. Their youngest son has already died from the looseness and only nine, he was.

Monday a beggar woman came with her two young sons. She was covered only by a filthy sack and her mouth was stained green from eating grass. I was in the field looking for herbs. I was thinking that the two boys might be up to no good. They had the wild eyes, darting this way and that, trying to see if anyone was around. Ma was alone in the house. Da was off in hopes of catching a fish.

The beggar woman sat down on a pile of stones to rest. She looked tired, and her face, 'twas as white as a cloud. The boys threw themselves into the pigsty and began gobbling up what the pigs had left.

Ma came out to see what the noise was about. She hollered for the boys to leave, but they just stood there. Finally their mother rose up from the pile of stones and told them to stop.

The woman turned to Ma and asked, "Is there a bit of bread for the hunger?" She said her husband had been killed by a runaway horse, and she held up her arms to show the loose skin hanging from her bones.

Ma told her she had nothing to spare and sent her on her way.

I dared not look Ma in the eye. I know how hard 'twas for her to send the poor woman away. Ma has always been the first to help a neighbor in need. Now all that has changed. We must watch out for ourselves.

Thursday, April 15, 1847
Skibbereen, County Cork, Ireland

It has been two weeks since Da killed the pigs. That was the last meal that could be named such.

What I wouldn't do for just one spoonful of potatoes and buttermilk.

'Tis food that fills my dreams at night — a big bowl overflowing with a bubbling stew. Thick chunks of fish bobbing up in between large pieces of carrots, onions, and turnips. I barely have time to give thanks. But when I lift the first spoonful to my mouth, one of the chunks of fish turns into the head of a terrible snapping turtle and bites my lip. I awake terribly hungry.

When I get to America, I will eat and eat and never stop.

Thursday, April 22, 1847
Skibbereen, County Cork, Ireland

I have bundled what little I have. I fear 'tis not enough. The voyage can take a month or more.

I have said my good-byes and called on every-one we know in the village.

Maureen said she will miss me dearly. She is as shy as a flower, that one. A true friend like her I will never find. Mr. Connelly talked about what life in America would be like. I don't know how he knows about America since he's never been out-side Skibbereen.

Mrs. Connelly made me some dried oatmeal cakes for the voyage. She said they will taste just fine dipped in hot tea. She gave me woolen stock-ings to keep my feet warm and a sleeping gown that closes in the front. Mrs. Connelly said that she was after speaking to any number of people, and she knows 'tis hard to lie in your sleeping berth and try to hook and eye from behind.

Not a word came from Da all night. He just sat there smoking his pipe. He's been like this since Kate left.

Father Mullaney provided the blessing.

By the time the Connellys and Father Mul-laney were gone, Ma's eyes were brimming with tears. She searched my face with a look so fierce I could feel the heat. I am thinking she wanted to make sure to remember what I looked like for fear we would not see each other again.

I sat down on the bed next to her. She held my face in her hands and smiled. She told me she would miss me awfully and that she had prayed to Sweet Jesus every night that we would not have to say good-bye. "But," she said, "these are terrible times, and there are too many sad memories here already."

I told her I was not afraid, although I surely was. She said 'tis a strange and far-off land I am going to, but to be sure, the Holy Mother of God will watch over me. "Remember," she said. "The Blessed Lord would never close one gate without opening another."

All that night Ma's words sounded over and over. How much I will miss her.

'Tis Mr. Nevin taking me in the morning. He still has his horse and cart. That way we do not have to walk the thirty miles to Cork.

We leave at first light.

Atlantic Ocean

Friday, April 30, 1847
Cork, Ireland

There are more people on this boat than in all of Skibbereen. I swear to Almighty God there are. They are everywhere — running every which way, carrying their cases and dragging their frightened children behind them. 'Tis all I can do to make sure I am not trampled underfoot.

There was quite a scare when we boarded. I was huddling against the inside wall of the ship with my bundle to my chest, and humming the lullaby Ma always sang to me when I was a wee girl:

> *On the wings of the wind*
> *Over the dark rolling deep*
> *Angels are coming*
> *To watch over thy sleep*

While I was humming, one of the crewmen came by carrying a long pole with a sharp nail sticking out of one end. He poked the stick into the dark corners of the ship and called out. Looking for something, he was.

Soon he was joined by two others who used hammers and chisels to break open some barrels. They turned one of them upside down. A man was hiding inside. He cried for help, and they let him out. He begged them to let him stay on the ship. Fell to his knees and pleaded for mercy, he did. Said he didn't have money for his ticket.

They laughed and put him ashore just the same.

I gripped my ticket tighter, pulled my bundle closer, and set out to find a place to sleep. The berths were jammed top to bottom. I feared there was no place on the ship for me.

I am thanking the Lord a man and his wife saw my sorry state and asked me to join them. Mr. and Mrs. O'Donnell are from Killarney. Mrs. O'Donnell has shiny red cheeks and blue, blue eyes like Ma. They are going to America to be with their daughter Alice. Mrs. O'Donnell says that Alice is almost my age — she is thirteen — and looks just like me. Mr. O'Donnell laughed. He told Mrs.

O'Donnell that Alice is surely pretty but couldn't compare with a "beauty" like me. His speech made me blush.

They are traveling with others from Killarney.

My sleeping berth is crudely made of splintery wood planks. The ceiling is so low, only the children around me are able to stand without hitting their heads on the underside of the deck. There are crawling things in every corner.

When we left port people rushed on to the main deck to say farewell to Ireland. What's done is done, I thought, and stayed below.

Thursday, May 6, 1847
At Sea

We must all sleep one above the other and within arm's length. I dare not undress to change into my sleeping gown. My berth is so narrow and uncomfortable, I must sleep on my side. 'Tis difficult to write down here.

Sunday, May 9, 1847
At Sea

The O'Donnells have been kind enough to share their food with me. Today we had butter and bread. If it were not for them, I would be hungry most of the time. My hard-boiled eggs and the oatmeal cakes are already gone. I was unable to get any tea for the oatmeal cakes and had to eat them as brittle as they were. The ship's crew provides little to eat besides these awful biscuits.

Tonight the O'Donnells cooked a stew with the Corcorans. Everyone eats from the same kettle. The rolling of the boat caused the kettle to sway. The stew spilled over the sides and put out the fire. Thankfully I do not suffer from seasickness like so many around me.

The Corcorans have two pretty twin girls — Molly and Sophie — and Brendan, who is nine.

I asked Mrs. Corcoran how old the twins were, and they shouted out, "Guess!" I pretended to give the question great consideration. "Three," I said, and they shook their heads, delighted that they had fooled me on my first guess. Again I appeared lost in thought. "Two?" This caused even greater delight. 'Twas true I was going off track, leaving them no choice but to tell me. They looked at each other, deciding who would tell. "Seven," Molly said. "My, my," I said. "I have never met twins that old. Never in all my days."

"I'm the oldest," Molly said proudly.

The whole while Brendan kept his distance. He doesn't trust me, that one, but that's just because I'm a girl.

Mrs. Corcoran is fine company. She is lovely to talk to and spends most of her time watching the children. Mr. Corcoran reminds me of Da, smoking his pipe and keeping to himself. When the weather is fair he plays cards on deck.

I went up with the Corcorans this morning to have water pumped into our cans from the large barrels on deck. 'Tis barely enough to satisfy our thirst, and there is hardly any left for cooking. We save the cooking water and use it to wash.

One of the barrels leaked and another was undrinkable because it once held vinegar. 'Tis a shame because there is not enough to waste.

There are only two privies for all of us. Both are above deck at the front of the ship. 'Tis impossible to use them without becoming soaked from the wind and the spray.

Worse than the long wait and the drenching are the rats that are always lurking about. Mrs. O'Donnell tells me to make as much noise as possible in order to scare them off. I do, but they don't seem to be too afraid.

Many take care of this below decks. There is a constant foul odor down there. In good weather, the main decks are so crowded during the day that 'tis difficult to find a place to stand.

Mrs. O'Donnell has offered me the use of their chamber pot. She is so kind to watch over me. She showed me how to keep it clean. Once a day now I go up on deck, tie the chamber pot to a rope, and empty it over the side. Then I dip it into the ocean and pull it back up by the rope. Glad, I am, to be a help in some way.

The twins have taken a liking to me. I tell them a story every morning now. It helps pass the time. They are more easily entertained than Brendan. The wee girls, especially Molly, are bolder than their brother. He is timid as a fawn, that one. This morning we played hide-and-seek. The girls raced down the cluttered aisles and found many clever places to hide. When I found them, they shrieked with joy. But I never could find Brendan's hiding place. He only came out after I had given up. Mrs. Corcoran thanked me for playing with the children. She said that this sorrowful voyage is hardest on them. I think so, too. There is nothing to occupy their time and much that is bewildering.

A violent gale began two days ago. The ship has been rolling awfully ever since. The wind whips around, and the storm-tossed sea bursts upon the decks with terrible force. The waves are so fierce that they rush down into the lower decks. Everything is closed off below to keep the water out. I expect at any moment for the ship to cave in, sending us to the bottom of the salt-sea ocean. 'Tis like a dark, airless dungeon down here. Lord knows I am frightened, but I do my best to hide my fears so the children won't be any worse for it.

Last night I could hear Brendan crying out my name. The Corcorans' sleeping berth is not far from mine. I made my way to him as best I could. 'Twas so dark, I tripped over people who shouted angrily at me. I whispered, "Brendan," as loud as I dared. Finally I heard, "Mary, over here."

Poor boy. He says he wants to go home. I explained that he is going to a *new* home. A *better* home. But he was having none of it. "Why," he cried, "can't we go to my old home? What's the matter with my old home?" Then he buried his head in my lap and cried himself to sleep while I sang to him softly:

> *On the wings of the night*
> *May your fury be crossed*
> *May no one that's dear*
> *To our island be lost*
>
> *Blow the winds gently*
> *Calm be the foam*
> *Shine the light brightly*
> *To guide them back home*

Thursday, May 13, 1847
At Sea

Three days now have I been forced to stay below because of the storm. I was kept awake by Mr. O'Donnell, who is suffering from the ship fever. He moans day and night and cries out for water. I made my way slowly over to their berth and asked Mrs. O'Donnell if there was anything I could do. She shook her head and squeezed my hand. I stayed with her for a bit, both of us silent. After a while I could stay down there no longer and went above.

The wind had stopped, though 'twas still raining as fast as it could. I crawled under a sail that lay on deck, hoping 'twould protect me. After a time I felt another leg touching mine. 'Twas a boy. Older than me, to be sure. But there was barely enough light to see. I couldn't tell if his eyes were open or closed. Didn't I think that he was sleeping or just keeping still. I prayed he wasn't dead.

We stayed like that for the longest time. I dared not move or make a sound. I hardly took a breath.

Finally he spoke. "I'm Sean Riordan," said he, as if that were something to be proud of. I told him my name. Then silence. The rain had stopped. He said we should come out from under the sail — now that the storm had passed. He had a cheerful voice.

He showed me how to stretch the sail so we could catch the rainwater in a water can. Moved like a cat, he did. Cautiously.

"I'm going to find work in America," he said.

His uncle Patrick Quinn sent the money for his ticket. He has been living in Boston for five years now. He owns a tavern.

I told Sean about Aunt Nora and my plans to work in the mills.

"Do they hire Irish?" he asked.

I must have made a queer face.

"Some places don't hire Irish, you know," he said.

Sean said that someday he would like to be rich. What would I do if I were rich? he was asking.

"I would bring Ma and Da to America," I told him.

"And then?" he went on. "What would you do then?"

I told him I would live in a big house on a cliff overlooking the ocean. And I would spend my days watching the waves come in while the seals sunned themselves on the rocks.

"And you?" I asked.

He thought carefully and looked away before talking. He said he would bring everyone from Ireland to America. "That would leave the English with what they deserve, a country with no peo-ple."

Suddenly I felt cold. "I must be off," I said. I had been away too long. I had to go below and see how Mr. O'Donnell was faring.

Sean wanted to lend a hand, but I said no, I thought it best I go alone.

Monday, May 17, 1847
At Sea

Mr. O'Donnell is still feverish.

I sat with Mrs. O'Donnell while she wiped his damp brow with a cloth. He sleeps most of the day, thank the Lord.

Mrs. O'Donnell is knitting a sweater for her daughter whom they haven't seen in two years. She is living with a family in Boston. Mrs. O'Don-nell says 'twas best for the child. 'Tis certain she misses Alice greatly. I think this is why she has been so kind to me.

She said it must have been hard for Ma to let me go to America. "'Tis hard for all the mothers," she said. The O'Donnells are eager to see their daughter again. "We will make it all up to her then," she said, though I am not sure of her meaning. She went on for some time. Mrs. O'Donnell says I am very patient for a wee girl. I suppose I am. I like listening to people, if that's what she means by patient. Besides, I told her, I'm not a wee girl. I'm fourteen.

Wednesday, May 19, 1847
At Sea

I can't write down below. 'Tis too dark, and I can find no peace. At least on deck 'tis light.

There are times during the night when I awake with the shivers and can't breathe. There is no air, and it feels as if there is a heavy weight sitting on my chest. When that happens I can never go back to sleep.

Thursday, May 20, 1847
At Sea

Mr. O'Donnell is worse each day. God bless him, there is no doctor on board. No one to turn to for help.

Friday, May 21, 1847
At Sea

Each morning when I hear Molly and Sophie coming, I pretend I am still sleeping. They scream and jump in my berth to wake me.

They are the first twins I have ever known. Just because they look alike you think they would be alike, but they are not. Sophie is quiet and serious and doesn't like to be away from her ma. Molly is more playful than her sister. Being with them helps with the boredom of the voyage and brings me the deepest joy.

Monday, May 24, 1847
At Sea

I am tired.

I fear I might fall over my own shadow. I can barely walk without stopping to catch my breath.

When Molly and Sophie came to wake me this morning they brought the bouncing balls Sean had found for them. But I couldn't play. I was too weak to even tell them a story. Sadly I had to send them back to Mrs. Corcoran.

Sean came to see me but I sent him away, too.

Wednesday, May 26, 1847
At Sea

I am dizzy. 'Tis a trial to write. I thought 'twas because of the hunger. This morning the dizziness was so bad I couldn't walk. My body is on fire. My throat is sore, and my lips dry and cracked.

I fear I have gotten the ship fever. First Mr. O'Donnell, and now will it take me, too?

'Twas nothing anyone could do for him. None of the crew is any help. Sean is right, they care nothing for us.

Mrs. O'Donnell is overcome with grief. She is not feeling well herself at all. She asked me to go with Mr. O'Donnell when they put him out to sea. She did not want him to be alone. Mrs. Corcoran and the children are staying below.

I did as she asked, although if truth be told, I was weak as a kitten. I was afraid. Sean came with me. We stood by as the crewmen wrapped Mr. O'Donnell in an old canvas sailcloth. They placed a great stone at his feet and sewed up the sailcloth. The ship's bells were tolling as he was slipped overboard into the sea.

I said a prayer for him before returning to my berth.

At Sea

At times I don't know if 'tis day or night down here. I sleep so poorly. There is little light from the one swinging lantern. 'Tis nearly impossible to write.

At Sea

The awful creaking of the timbers. All night long.

By my faith, maybe I won't live to see America. Maybe Aunt Nora is wrong.

'Tis a long voyage, and I feel so far from home.

Monday, May 31, 1847
At Sea

I miss the children. Sean says they are asking why they can't see me. They want to know when I'll be all better.

Sean brought me some tea and a slice of bread with sugar on top.

'Tis a miracle because there is little food left and no tea. But a friend of Sean's uncle gave him some whiskey before he departed. To be sure, it has come in handy. Sean traded the whiskey for the tea and bread. Said the cook was most happy with the trade, thinking he had gotten the better of the deal. I laughed. I can't remember the last time I laughed.

Merciful Son of God, I have been spared.

My fever has passed.

Sean said he feared I would not recover. "The Holy Ghost looks after me," I told him.

We all went up on deck where Sean played his

fiddle. Sophie, Molly, and Brendan held hands and danced round and round while Mr. and Mrs. Corcoran clapped. Two of the sailors were tapping their feet as they mended the sails and tarred the ropes.

'Twas raining lightly, and Mr. Corcoran put his pipe upside down to keep it dry. Just like Da.

Monday, June 7, 1847
At Sea

The good Lord God took Mrs. O'Donnell today. 'Twas the ship fever. Once Mr. O'Donnell died she seemed to give up all hope.

I told Sean that somehow I had to find Alice O'Donnell when we arrived in Boston. The O'Donnells looked after me like I was their own. I must repay their kindness.

I can't bear the thought that the poor child will never see them again. She must know all they went through to be with her. 'Twas so sad it made me cry, something I never do.

I don't like to cry.

Tuesday, June 8, 1847
At Sea

There is a man selling dolls. How I wished we were able to get one for Molly and Sophie. 'Twould so help make their time pass more pleasantly.

Wednesday, June 9, 1847
At Sea

Sean came to see us this morning. He had something behind his back and a big grin on his face. The twins knew whatever he had was for them. They tried to see what it might be while Sean twisted this way and that. Molly and Sophie squealed with delight when Sean finally gave them the doll. I dare not ask where he got it.

Today Brendan said that Sean is going to teach him how to whistle.

Thursday, June 10, 1847
At Sea

The weather was fair today, and the captain allowed lines to be strung between the masts. I helped Mrs. Corcoran with the wash. We had to use sea water, which gives no suds. We did the best we could, beating the clothes against the decks. Mrs. Corcoran told me to be sure to shake them out once they were dry. This is to rid the salt from the sea water. She said they would burn our skin if we didn't.

Friday, June 11, 1847
At Sea

Mr. Corcoran was beaten by one of the crew two days ago. He lies in his berth all day and isn't speaking. No one knows what happened.

Sean heard one of the crew talking about Mr. Corcoran. He was found smoking his pipe below decks. Sean says the crewman talked about a fire aboard another ship earlier this year. The fire was put out and the ship returned to Cork. No one was hurt. 'Twas started by someone smoking in his berth. Just like Mr. Corcoran. There have been reports of fires on other ships bound for America. Ships that were lost at sea, with everyone perishing.

I am sorry for Mr. Corcoran, but not sorry his smoking below decks has stopped. Imagine the whole lot of us sinking because Mr. Corcoran was smoking his pipe.

Sean put aside water so that we can wash before we reach Boston. We barely have enough to drink, down to a cup a day, we are, so it seems fool-ish to worry about washing. But Sean says his uncle warned him that your troubles are not over once you've reached harbor. If the authorities think you are ill, they will place you in quarantine or worse, send you back to Ireland.

The thought of being returned to Ireland after all this time and all I've been through is more than I can bear.

Thursday, June 17, 1847
At Sea

There is talk we are nearing land.

Many of the passengers are buying tickets for the lottery. They are trying to see who can guess when land will be sighted. A ticket is sold for each hour of the day. Those who have tickets for days past try to buy tickets for upcoming days. Tickets for daylight hours fetch the highest price. Espe-cially the early-morning hours, when land is most likely to be spotted. Whoever has the winning ticket gets all the money.

Friday, June 18, 1847
At Sea

The ship is buzzing with excitement. Word is spreading like wildfire.

Mr. Corcoran has heard the rumors that we are nearing America. Now he stands on deck all day, one hand holding his ticket, the other the railing. He stares straight ahead, waiting. I don't know where he gets the strength.

Sunday, June 20, 1847
At Sea

Sean saw seaweed floating on the surface of the ocean.

We are indeed nearing land. Sweet Jesus, it's been so long, I dare not hope.

At long last, land.
Just saying the word. Land.
I feel like I've been on this ship for all eternity.

Lowell, Massachusetts

Glory be to God.

'Tis true.

America.

You could see it.

Everyone who could walk rushed up on deck, bringing their bundles and their cases with them. Many fell to their knees and gave thanks to the Lord in heaven. Others wept and embraced those around them as tears ran down their cheeks.

'Tis over, this horrible voyage is over.

My new life is about to begin. I give thanks to the Lord who mercifully granted me the good fortune to see this day.

Many were not so fortunate.

Wednesday, June 23, 1847
Boston

So much has happened. I must try to write.

When the medical officer and the other men

boarded the ship, the celebration ended. Everyone crowded together on deck, thinking the nearness would protect us.

The men stretched ropes across the ship so that there was only enough room for one person at a time to walk. They went to calling out names. Those whose names were called walked between the ropes to where the medical officer stood waiting. And quickly he worked. Those he judged healthy were allowed to leave. Those he thought ill or feverish were stopped and questioned.

One wee boy was found to be infected. His mother begged to remain with him. But her pleas were for naught. The boy was too sick to even cry out and was carried away. 'Twas his poor mother they held back. But little enough could they do to hold back her shrieks, which stabbed the air.

I tried not to watch but my eyes were fixed, like a moth to the flame.

Saddest of all were the Corcorans. First the medical officer examined the twins and Brendan. 'Tis a miracle the children have never had a day's sickness since the voyage began. Mrs. Corcoran looked drained but was not feverish. They were allowed to pass.

Then came Mr. Corcoran. He was having trouble standing. The medical officer was asking him questions but no answer was coming. He wasn't even looking at the officer. Looking right past him, he was, to America. He was still clutching his losing lottery ticket in his hand.

Suddenly he was pushed to the side and before anything could be done, he was led away. I began to move forward to help, but Sean was grabbing my arm. Mrs. Corcoran looked confused. Everything was happening so fast.

"Be on your way!" one of the men shouted. Mrs. Corcoran carried Sophie, while Brendan took Molly by the hand, and they made their way down to the wharf.

How will they find each other? I thought. What will happen to Mr. Corcoran? Where was he being taken?

"Mary Driscoll," the man called out.

"Go," Sean whispered. "Be brave."

Trembling, I was, while the doctor looked in my

eyes. He asked me to open my mouth and hold out my tongue. I prayed that I showed no signs of the fever. He was standing close and looking at me. His eyes were coal black and as hard as flint. Afraid to look at him, I was, but afraid not to. If I looked away he would think I did have something to hide.

Finally he looked down, wrote something on a piece of paper, put a blue tag on my shawl, and told me to move along.

Sean said to wait and not to let anyone help me no matter what. His uncle warned him that the runners will steal from you or try to take you to one of the boardinghouses. Then they will demand to be paid for their service. "America," he said, "is no place for a fool."

I waited for Sean while keeping a sharp eye out for Aunt Nora.

'Twas chaos all around me. Passengers streaming off the boat, people being greeted by their families and friends. 'Twas a scene of wildest excitement, I promise you that. Everyone running after one thing or the other. I didn't see how Aunt Nora would ever find me. But I stayed rooted to the spot just the same.

Suddenly a man appeared out of nowhere.

He snatched the bundle from my arms and told me he would be pleased to find me proper lodgings.

"We have no need of your services," someone behind me was saying. 'Twas Sean and with him, his uncle. Mr. Quinn was not as tall as Sean, but as thick as a stone wall, he was. His face wore a terrible look. He told the man we didn't need aid of any kind from the likes of him. Praise God, the man dropped the bundle, turned, and disappeared into the crowd.

I was still not seeing Aunt Nora. The docks had emptied. Only a few sailors and stragglers were still about. The sky was turning dark. "We must leave soon," Sean was saying. Where was it but to Aunt Nora's that I had to go? Why she was not there to meet me only God can say. What would I do? I didn't even know Kate's address.

I couldn't leave until Aunt Nora came. "Go on without me," I said. "I will be all right."

Sean said he would not be going without me. He would stay all night if waiting was my choice. "But," he said, "'tis a foolish thing to do."

Sean's uncle said 'twas not likely my aunt would be coming at this late hour. Missed connections are common now that so many Irish are coming to America. Sometimes a ship is late or a letter gets lost. He promised to place a notice in the Irish newspaper. "All will turn out well in the end, young lady," he assured me.

Mr. Quinn urged me to allow him to take me to his home for some food and a good night's rest. I was hungry and tired to the bone. I was sorely in need of shelter for the night. "'Tis a long road that has no turning," he said gently.

I accepted his kind offer.

The roads are not paved with gold as Aunt Nora said. I asked Sean's uncle if we would be coming upon them soon, and he laughed heartily.

There is so much to see and hear. The tall houses with their spires and chimney tops are piled one on top of the other. Everything is bigger than back in Skibbereen. The roads are filled with people rushing around, moving so fast — and all at the same time. Not one slowed to rest. Carts and carriages of every shape and size drive wildly, their warning bells ringing out. No one pays any mind.

They barely look before stepping into the road, the carriages flying past their noses.

Everywhere I looked there were Irish. 'Tis a wonder there are any of us left in Ireland. They seemed as worn and hungry as those I left behind in Skibbereen. Some were begging for food. Some were standing on the street corners. Still others simply stared out from doorways. Far from the kings and queens I expected to see dressed in their robes of red.

Friday, June 25, 1847
Boston

Sean's uncle was able to find out where Alice O'Donnell was living from a man he knows at his tavern. 'Tis a miracle if you ask me. We found the building, but there were so many rooms we didn't know where to begin.

Finally a man came out and told Mr. Quinn that Alice O'Donnell was in the cellar. She earned her keep doing the wash for a family with a flock of children that lives upstairs.

God help her, the poor child was curled up asleep on a mattress when we found her. 'Twas so damp, the mattress was soaked and her clothes were wet. Not a ray of light and precious little air to breathe down there.

When Mr. Quinn woke her, she opened her eyes wide. I could see the fear within. I reached for her, hoping she would take my hand. She made no move. 'Twasn't because of the fear. The poor child could not see.

Why Mrs. O'Donnell did not tell me her daughter was blind only the Lord can say. Her conditions, along with the state she was living in, grieved me terribly.

Mr. Quinn kept his wits about him. He told Alice O'Donnell we were her friends and we had come to help her. He asked if she could speak, but she said not a word. 'Twas plain for all to see she was horribly treated. Mr. Quinn and Sean left to find the family she worked for, while I tried to talk to her.

Alice O'Donnell remained crouched in the corner, her knees up to her chin, holding herself and rocking. I wanted dearly to find the right words to say. I wanted to tell her I knew her family and that she could trust me, but wasn't I afraid. How would I answer if she asked where they were? When they would be coming for her?

Gently I touched her hand, but she pulled back. I tried again, but still she withdrew. I didn't know if I were scaring her more than she already was. 'Twas then I decided to sing, hoping Ma's lullaby might soothe her:

> *On the wings of the wind*
> *Over the dark rolling deep*
> *Angels are coming*
> *To watch over thy sleep*
>
> *Angels are coming*
> *To watch over thee*
> *So list' to the wind*
> *Coming over the sea*
>
> *Hear the wind blow*
> *Hear the wind blow*
> *Lean your head over*
> *Hear the wind blow*

Still singing, I tried once more to touch her hands. I could see that some of the fear had fallen from her eyes. This time she let me stroke her fingers and press her hands in mine. She was listening carefully now to every sound. I could tell by the way she cocked her head. Slowly she reached out with her other hand and searched the air for my face. I leaned forward, and she found my chin. Then she felt for my mouth and my eyes. She stroked my hair, trying to see how long 'twas.

Then we both heard steps. 'Twas Sean and his uncle. Alice's hand remained in mine.

I don't know what Mr. Quinn said to the family, but when he returned he was pacing up and down like a caged animal. He said that Alice O'Donnell would be leaving with us. She would stay with him and his wife until it could be decided what was best for her. Then he looked at me. I wasn't sure what he wanted me to do.

I told Alice that we were her friends. That I had just come from Ireland. She felt my face again. I told her my name and promised that no harm would come to her.

She was tilting her head again. I wished she would talk to me. She moved her hand across my face, feeling the tears falling down my cheeks. "My name is Alice," she said in a whisper, and we stood up to leave.

Thursday, July 8, 1847
Lowell

Aunt Nora never received the letter telling her what ship I would be on. 'Twas only when she saw the notice in *The Pilot* — the one placed by Mr. Quinn — that she knew I was in America and sent Kate to get me.

As soon as Kate arrived at Mr. Quinn's, she made it plain that she was wanting to leave. So I hurried along as best I could.

Aunt Nora was unable to come herself. The journey would be too much for her bad leg. If only I had known 'twas Kate coming in her place, I would have found a way to get to Lowell on my own, to be sure.

" 'Tis glad I am to see my little sister after all

this time," Kate said. But she appeared to be no more glad about it than I.

The stagecoach ride to Lowell was a rocky one. The two men who journeyed with us seemed to welcome Kate's chatter. My sister still talks without end, choosing to use two words when one would do. Her favorite subject is still herself.

In that way Kate has changed little in the past two years. But she looks and sounds like a different girl. She fixes her hair in a braided crown now and dresses with great care. (She was wearing a fancy white dress.) She speaks with a wee singsong voice that sounds make-believe — like she were a fairy-tale princess. Everyone was always fooled by that round, milk-white, innocent-looking face, even Ma. But not me. My sister has two faces — one she wears on the outside, and one she wears when she thinks no one is looking. I can see she has taken easily to the ways of this new world. 'Tisn't surprising.

She went on and on about Mrs. Abbott. Mrs. Abbott and her children are visiting relatives in Philadelphia. Mr. Abbott is the agent for the Merrimack Mills. 'Tis thanks to him I will be working there. Kate said it was very kind of Mrs. Abbott to allow her to travel all the way to Boston to "fetch" me — like I were the hen for that night's supper. Proud, she is, that Mrs. Abbott favors her above the others. Mrs. Abbott considers Kate to be trustworthy. "Unlike other Irish," my sister said.

When she first went to work for Mrs. Abbott, she was cleaning and discovered a dollar under one of the beds. Kate had been warned that this was something Yankee women do. Mrs. Abbott had placed the dollar there on purpose — just to see if Kate would be tempted. That afternoon she gave her the dollar, telling Mrs. Abbott that someone must have accidentally dropped it under the bed and that she hoped Mrs. Abbott would be able to return it to its rightful owner.

"Aren't you an angel," Mrs. Abbott told Kate.

Kate lectured me about all the things Mrs. Abbott has taught her: how to set the table, where to place the wineglasses. She has learned how to polish fruit properly and arrange flowers. Kate says Mrs. Abbott likes everything just so. I would think she does.

There are times when Mrs. Abbott speaks to Kate like a friend. My sister is quite proud of this.

Mrs. Abbott also employs two cooks and a lady from England who looks after the Abbott children.

'Twas dark when we arrived in Lowell. We went in the back door and up the stairs — Mrs. Abbott does not allow the servants to use the front door — and down the hall to Kate's room.

Kate said that Aunt Nora picked a fine time to take to bed. 'Tis a great burden for her to take me to the mills in the morning, that much is plain. I don't know what to do. I would go myself, to be sure, but I don't know where they are or how to get there. We are going to see Mr. Fowler. He works for Mr. Abbott as the overseer.

I awoke at dawn. The early morning light was just beginning to come through the window. Not even a bird was awake. I was terribly confused. 'Twas like I was in a dream. I wanted to find a place to write because so much has happened.

Slowly I left the bed, being sure not to disturb Kate, who was still asleep in the bed beside me. I opened the door and went into the hall. I stopped and listened, but heard no sound other than my own breathing.

I found myself standing in front of the door that leads to Mrs. Abbott's bedchamber. Mrs. Abbott is away, I remembered Kate saying. No one would be in there. My curiosity was greater than my fear. I went in.

The room is big. A wide, white bed that has a white cloth stretched above it is in one corner. It looks like a heavenly carriage. Opposite the bed is a window framed by folds of blue shiny cloth. I parted the cloth and looked down on a beautiful garden enclosed by a white fence. This, I thought, must be what a garden in paradise looks like. *This* is what I pictured America to be.

The walls of the room are covered with paper. Different pleasant scenes are shown: animals in the forest, flowers in the field, and a picnic by the lake. Along one wall where the picnic is, I saw the most comfortable-looking ruby-red cushioned chair. I ran my hand over the cloth. 'Twas soft — like the fur of a baby animal. I sat down carefully and put my arms on the arms of the chair. I felt like a queen. I wondered what 'twould be like to live in this house.

Across the room is a tall chest of drawers with an oval mirror framed in swirling dark wood on top.

I went over to it. Lying on the top was a box made of different woods, some light, some dark. They were put together in a way that made a pattern. 'Twas an A for Abbott. The wood was smoother than any I have ever seen or touched. The box gleamed like still water reflecting the moonlight. What treasures, I wondered, would be kept in such a precious box? I hesitated, but I could not stop myself. I opened the box, not knowing what to expect.

Will you look at that, I thought. Jewelry. Lying on the rose-colored cloth within were shiny rings, golden bracelets, strings of pearls, and red and green necklaces. Even in the weak light of the coming dawn the contents of the glorious box shimmered, sparkly and golden. I gently pulled out a long, silver necklace with square green stones dangling along its length. I put it around my neck and looked in the mirror. I saw my face for the first time in a long while. My, how thin I look. I touched my cheeks. There is barely any skin on my bones.

What if these were my jewels and 'twas *I* who was preparing to dress for the evening?

Then I heard something.

The floorboards above were creaking. Someone was up and about. I closed the box and held my breath. I stood frozen, unable to move. What if someone heard me? Or saw me come into the room? What would they do to me? Why had I come in here? I should have known better.

Be still, a voice within me warned. I knew that if I were found out there would be the devil to pay. Perhaps 'twas just someone stirring in the night. Perhaps 'twas my imagination. I had heard nothing since. I was afraid to leave the room, but I knew the longer I stayed the worse 'twould be. The sky was growing lighter with every moment I delayed.

I turned the doorknob slowly and pulled the door toward me. Thank the Lord, it made no sound.

Being careful to close the door behind me I, tiptoed quietly and quickly down the hall and back to the room before anyone saw me. Kate, praise God, was still sleeping soundly. I crouched down by the window to get the light. I am writing quickly, not knowing how long 'twill be before my sister awakes.

Friday, July 9, 1847
Lowell

Mrs. Abbott's house is so near the mills we were able to walk there. On the way Kate reminded me to be polite and respectful.

I told her I hoped I would be acceptable, which caused her to laugh.

She said I should not concern myself with that. "The Yankee girls are leaving faster than they are coming," she said. "Mr. Abbott is eager to replace them with as many Irish girls as he can because the Irish won't complain about things the way the Yankee girls do."

What "things"? I wondered, but spoke not a word.

The bright redbrick building is so tall, it seems to reach the sky. I never dreamed earthly hands could make anything that big. It looked to me like all the people in Ireland could fit inside. 'Twas like a fortress. There were smokestacks blowing their blackness heavenward and darkening the sky.

I felt cold although the day was warm. A shudder rippled through my body. There is nothing to be afraid of, I told myself. What could be worse than what I had already seen back in Ireland?

I had to go through those gates.

The guard led us to see Mr. Fowler. He is the oddest-looking man. Bald as a crow, he is. The sunlight from the window above fell on his hairless head, causing it to glow.

Kate told him that I was Mary Driscoll, the girl Mr. Abbott mentioned. I think she was ashamed to say I was her sister. Mr. Fowler looked at me like that doctor did in Boston Harbor. I wonder, does everyone in America look at you this way?

Could I write my name? he asked. I told him I could. He handed me a paper and showed me where to sign, which I did without reading what it said. I was too afraid.

I start Monday in spinning room number three.

Kate left just as soon as she delivered me to Aunt Nora. "Only Irish live in the Acre," she said as we neared. 'Tis plain she doesn't like being in this part of Lowell. In such a rush, she was, that her heels nearly touched her head when she left.

The Acre is not far from the mills but it might as well be on the other side of the ocean. The roads are narrow, twisting, and muddy — not like the roads where Mrs. Abbott lives. The houses are crowded together, and goats, geese, chickens, and pigs roam everywhere. There are no houses such as Mrs. Abbott's in the Acre.

There must be two Lowells. One where Mrs. Abbott lives and one where Aunt Nora lives.

Perhaps there are two Americas.

'Twas sad to see that Aunt Nora uses a cane because of her bad leg. "Don't let it trouble you, child," she said when I asked her how she was feeling. "First come and give us a hug. Hasn't it been ever so long a time. I've missed you terrible. Why, bless us and save us, Quiet One, 'tis a pure joy to behold your angelic face. How lovely you've become. I've been as lonely as a church mouse these past six years. But now that you are here I'll be lonely no more."

Seeing Aunt Nora made me feel safe for the first time since I left home.

I am glad my coming to America is a help and not a burden.

I held back the tears from my eyes. Aunt Nora said that she knew it must be hard but that we would care for each other.

Just then the Delaneys came home. They are Aunt Nora's boarders.

Mrs. Delaney is old. Her face wears a thousand wrinkles, and her hair looks matted and dirty. Her son, John, looks like he wouldn't say boo to a goose.

"She's afflicted with the kind of complaint no one can understand," Aunt Nora said after they had gone into the other room.

Mrs. Delaney helps Aunt Nora care for the two pigs. Once in a while she gives a good sweeping to the kitchen. Mr. Delaney disappeared two years ago, and she and John have been staying with Aunt Nora ever since.

"Mr. Delaney was the laziest rogue that ever wore clothes and was fed," Aunt Nora said. She thinks Mrs. Delaney is better off without him. "Now he won't be pourin' the family's money down his throat all day. But she was left with a heavy handful."

It's her son, John, that Aunt Nora calls a heavy handful. "The boy's a little daft, though not totally useless. 'Twas him that whitewashed the cottage. And all by himself I might add. But he acts like something that fell of a tinker's cart and was never missed."

John seems harmless just the same. He has found work north of here. He leaves in the morning. My aunt can be a harsh judge when she has a mind to.

There are only two rooms. The Delaneys sleep on the floor in one and Aunt Nora and me in the bed in the kitchen. Beside the bed there are two benches, a table, and a rocking chair near the fireplace. Aunt Nora is proud of the large stone fireplace at the end of the room. She said 'tis a great comfort come winter. Winters can be fierce, she says. There is only one tiny window to let light in.

Aunt Nora urged me to go to bed. I told her I wanted to talk some more. I wanted to tell her about Alice O'Donnell. She said I could barely keep my head up, which was a fact, and that there would be plenty of time tomorrow.

Saturday, July 10, 1847
Lowell

'Twas the best night's sleep I've had in a long, long time.

I dreamed Molly and Sophie were safe at home. But not Brendan. I didn't know where he was and decided to look for him. 'Twas getting darker by the minute. I didn't want to leave the twins alone, but I had no choice. I had a serious talk with them. Got down on one knee, I did, so I could look both in the eyes. I told them I was going to look for Brendan. That he should have been home by now. They nodded like they understood but they can fool you, those little ones. I told them they had to promise not to leave and not to open the door for anyone, no matter what. I got up, put on my cloak, and wrapped it tight around me, for the night was cold. I turned to take one last look at their shiny faces. They smiled and said, "No matter what, Mary, no matter what," and then giggled. Then I awoke.

Aunt Nora was sitting in her rocking chair. It took me a while to remember where I was. Mrs. Delaney and her son were nowhere to be seen, praise God. I so wanted to talk to Aunt Nora about Alice O'Donnell.

I was only going to say a little. But once I began there was no stopping me. It just came spilling out. Aunt Nora, bless her heart, listened patiently while I told her the sad tale.

When I was done she asked if Mr. Quinn knew what had happened to cause the poor girl to find herself so all alone. I told her that he thought she must have come to America with someone. That her family must not have been able to care for her properly back in Ireland. They must have believed she would be better off in America. I remember Mrs. O'Donnell saying that. That 'twould be for the best. Mr. Quinn thinks whoever was with Alice O'Donnell did not survive the passage.

I told Aunt Nora that I could not bring myself to tell Alice about her ma and da. I pray that I made the right decision.

Sunday, July 11, 1847
Lowell

I don't have to go to church today. Aunt Nora said 'tis better I rest.

I am to be at the mills by five-thirty tomorrow morning. If I am late the main gates will be closed and I will have to enter through the counting house.

'Twould not be good to be late on my first day.

Monday, July 12, 1847
Lowell

Spinning room number three takes up the whole floor. There are long rows of machines lined up, one next to the other, as far as the eye can see. There are girls tending to them up and down the aisles. I cannot say how many machines there are, but there must be hundreds. Of that I am certain. Each was making the most awful hissing and whizzing sounds. This devilish noise came rushing down all around me like an endless water-fall. The sound was so great that the floor beneath my feet trembled. I could feel the thunderous sound come up my legs. I feared I would cry out and run from the room, just to be rid of it. God help me.

Mr. Fowler said that one of the girls would teach me my tasks. 'Twas nearly impossible to hear what he was saying. He had to holler right into my ear. He pulls on his red mustache and mops his damp brow with a handkerchief while he talks.

He warned me not to daydream. 'Tis important to pay strict attention at all times and not to hold up the girls.

I spied one of the Yankee girls watching me while Mr. Fowler yelled into my ear. She gave me quite a start. Seeing her was like looking into a mirror. She has the same green eyes and the same honey-red hair I do. Lucky girl, she does not have freckles. She looks older, maybe seventeen. Most of the girls look older than me.

The girl looked at me in a gentle way. (Many of the girls were not looking at me so gently.) My prayers were answered when Mr. Fowler called her over. She was waiting for his signal. Her name is Annie Clark. Mr. Fowler left us alone and returned to his desk at the far end of the room. He walks with his hands held behind his back, standing stiff and straight, like he must have swallowed a crowbar.

Annie Clark explained that I am to be a bobbin girl. She showed me the wooden crates on rollers where the empty bobbins are kept and how to doff the bobbins when they are filled with the spun yarn. Then I take them off the spinning frame and replace them quickly with empty ones. I must hurry so the spinning frames are not stopped long. While there are no bobbins to change, I can sit quietly and wait.

There are four or five other Irish girls who do the same thing. The others are Yankee girls.

A bell rang in the middle of the day, and Annie

said she would be going to dinner. She showed me where I could sit outside.

I watched her join the other Yankee girls who were streaming back into their boardinghouses while I ate the hard-boiled egg Aunt Nora had fixed. The girls are as fine as fine, one prettier than the next. And they wear the sweetest dresses. I wish I had something to wear besides these rags.

The boardinghouses are made of redbrick, just like the mills, but they are much smaller. There is row upon row of them, lined up neatly just across the canal. They are pretty, just like the girls who live there. I wonder what 'tis like inside.

Friday, July 16, 1847
Lowell

I have been too tired to write. Perhaps I will be able to on Sunday, my only day of rest.

Sunday, July 18, 1847
Lowell

Went to St. Patrick's for the first time with Aunt Nora. She sings in the choir, and 'tis a beautiful voice she has.

Tuesday, July 20, 1847
Lowell

A letter from Sean.

He and his uncle have found a convent in Arlington where Alice will be cared for. Mr. Quinn believes she is in the proper hands now, and he will keep watch over her.

Sean has had difficulty finding work. His first job was a long way from Boston. So many Irish were seeking work there that the promised wages were lowered to sixty-five cents a day. Sean said they had to take what was offered. There were plenty of men ready to take their places.

Sean found work in Somerville. The wages are

better, but the work is difficult due to the heat of the day and the swamp nearby.

He gives me no address. I do have Mr. Quinn's address in Boston so I can write him if necessary. I am glad that Alice O'Donnell is safe. By now she must know about her ma and da. Before I left Boston, Mr. Quinn asked me what I had decided, to tell Alice or not. Truth is I hadn't decided anything. I think Mr. Quinn could see that. "Leave it in my hands," he had said, and I was glad to do just that.

Saturday, July 24, 1847
Lowell

Kate visited today. She was having tea with Aunt Nora when I returned from the mills. Saturday work is only a half day.

As always Kate had much news about herself.

In three weeks she is going away with Mrs. Abbott to visit Mrs. Abbott's sister. She lives in Boston but spends her summers in Rhode Island. Mrs. Abbott has decided to join her because 'tis near the ocean and therefore much cooler.

Kate boasts about how much Mrs. Abbott needs her. Yankee ladies, she says, know that good help is precious. Kate thinks being a servant for a rich lady is better than being a mill girl. She thinks that if she works for Mrs. Abbott and lives in Mrs. Abbott's house she can act like Mrs. Abbott.

Aunt Nora says that Kate's head has swelled quite a bit since she came to America.

Mill work suits me just fine, 'twas all I said. I didn't want her to know that my bones ache, my ankles swell up, and my body throbs from head to toe at night. I didn't tell her that the spinning room is so noisy, I think it must be what hell itself sounds like.

Still, I prefer work in the mills. Once I am done, my time, such that 'tis, is my own.

Monday, July 26, 1847
Lowell

Aunt Nora's leg is on the mend.

Poor dear. It has never truly healed since she

tumbled on the rocks back home. But she is going around now without a cane.

My heart is filled with joy. When I got home Aunt Nora was waiting with a letter from Skibbereen.

('Tis Father Mullaney who writes Ma's letters.)

She sends greetings from the Connellys. Maureen wishes she could be here with me. Not nearly as much as I do. Sadly Mr. and Mrs. Sweeney have fallen victim to the black fever. 'Twas to be expected. They were so very ill when I left.

Ma and Da have not been evicted from our cottage, thanks to the kindness of Mr. Hughes, the landlord.

I pray to the Heavenly Father each night that they will keep well even though they face great hardship. I pray I will be able to earn enough money to send for them before 'tis too late.

Friday, July 30, 1847
Lowell

Annie Clark spoke to me today. I have learned my tasks quickly and well. She said she is very proud of me, which made me blush, I'm sure. There is a need for another spinner, just like her, if I am interested. Spinning means I will be paid more money. So I said yes, I would like to be a spinner. Annie is going to speak to Mr. Fowler.

Monday, August 2, 1847
Lowell

Mrs. Delaney cries in the night because she has not heard from her son. I wish she wouldn't cry. It makes me think back to the nights I heard Ma crying.

Tuesday, August 3, 1847
Lowell

'Tis raining again today. Rain all week.

Thursday, August 5, 1847
Lowell

Aunt Nora can put a fright into you if she has a mind to. She had a row with Mr. Byrnes, who is also a teacher at St. Patrick's.

She says Mr. Byrnes hit wee Liam O'Neil, one of the students. Mr. Byrnes got it into his head that Liam was making fun of him behind his back. Liam said he did not, but Mr. Byrnes hit him a number of times with a heavy strap.

Aunt Nora said he has no call to be carrying on like that, and she's going to make him scratch where he doesn't itch.

Friday, August 6, 1847
Lowell

Annie Clark has spoken to Mr. Fowler. He is going to allow me to become a spinner. Annie has been very patient with me. She showed me carefully how to tend the spinning frame. I am to watch for breaks in the yarn. If there is a break, the machine stops. I piece together the two ends of the yarn with a small, special knot that Annie showed me how to tie. Then I am to restart the spinning frame.

Annie won't leave me on my own until I am ready. God bless her.

Saturday, August 7, 1847
Lowell

I told Aunt Nora the good news. She is proud of me, too.

After Mass I went for a walk in the woods near the canal. I came upon Annie Clark. I think we were both surprised. I would have liked to turn away, but the narrowness of the path did not allow for that.

"Good morning, Mary Driscoll," she said.

We discovered that this is our favorite path. In weeks past we must have missed each other only by a matter of minutes.

We fell to talking easily. Annie told me she thinks I am "catching on nicely." That's how she put it — "catching on nicely." She has such a fine way of talking. I told her that I was nervous at first, but that I am feeling more comfortable each day. She is going to leave me on my own soon.

She wanted to know if I missed Ireland, if 'twas hard coming to a new country, if I liked America. So many questions. Truth is I'm not certain, not yet, about America. And that's what I told her. She said I was a spunky one when I told her that.

Annie comes from the state of Maine. I asked her if *she* misses home. She doesn't. She likes being on her own.

'Twas late afternoon before I knew it. The air had turned cold and damp.

Annie has invited me to supper at her boardinghouse next Sunday. I said yes, but now I have only regrets. What will I say? What will I wear? Annie always dresses so prettily, as do the other girls, and my clothes are so ragged.

I told Aunt Nora about going to Annie Clark's boardinghouse. She says I should worry about tomorrow tomorrow. 'Tis good advice, but I'm not sure I'm up to it.

Friday, August 13, 1847
Lowell

Mr. Byrnes, the teacher who hit Liam O'Neill, was found dead yesterday morning. He fell from the roof of St. Patrick's. 'Tis a mystery what he was doing up there or how he fell.

Aunt Nora sang a tune all evening while I helped her cut and peel the potatoes.

Sunday, August 15, 1847
Lowell

All the boardinghouses on Dutton Street look the same. Annie's is the sixth one from the corner, so I counted and knocked. I hummed while I waited, and I prayed for the Blessed Virgin to help me.

The door was opened by Mrs. Jackson, the boardinghouse keeper.

She took me by the arm and pulled me into the hall, saying I could use some flesh on my bare bones.

The bonnets and shawls that all the Yankee girls wear hung neatly from the hooks on the hallway wall. Near them was a list of the rules the girls were to follow.

"My girls," Mrs. Jackson said, "are just now coming down." Indeed they were. Doors were slamming closed, and I could hear them on the stairs. All the girls seemed to be talking at once. Sounded like a flock of screaming seagulls, they did.

When I saw Annie, she squeezed my hand and whispered, "Just do as I do." I hurried along and sat down next to her at one of the two large tables the girls were crowding around. They began passing large platters of boiled beef, potatoes, and steaming bowls of cabbage and vegetables. Everyone helped themselves to bread and crackers and gobbled down their food faster than I thought possible.

American girls do everything quickly.

They were all dressed with care and fixed their hair so neatly. I don't know how they do it. Annie was wearing a plain blue dress and black slippers. Many of the girls were dressed fancier than Annie, but none shone as brightly. Like a fairy-tale princess, she is.

Annie introduced me to the other girls at the table. Ruth Shattuck, Eunice Currier, Laura Austin, and Clarissa Burroughs. I have seen Clarissa Burroughs before, with Annie.

'Twas that first day, I remember now, when Annie showed me where I could eat. Clarissa Burroughs was watching us. But she didn't see me seeing her.

Ruth, Eunice, and Laura are all kindly in manner. You could tell they were trying to make me feel at home.

Laura asked how I like mill work. 'Tis fine, I told her. She has a steady gaze, and her eyes can bore a hole through you. She wanted to know what is fine about it. Truth is I was hoping not to have to do much talking. Not with all those finely dressed Yankee girls listening. But Laura's voice was as calm and steady as her gaze. I knew she wouldn't be satisfied until I told her.

So I explained that the mills paid steady and good, and that I plan to earn enough money to send for Ma and Da.

That made Clarissa Burroughs laugh. I know the Yankee girls think I talk funny.

Laura Austin went on as if nothing had happened.

She said she can see why Annie likes me. 'Twas nice of her to say, especially in front of the other girls. I think Laura Austin was being nice because of Clarissa Burroughs.

Ruth asked if 'tis hard with all the new things I have to learn. I said that Annie is a good and patient teacher, which made Ruth laugh, though not the way Clarissa Burroughs did. Ruth was Annie's teacher when Annie first came to the mills.

Then Ruth got a faraway look in her eyes. Did I miss being home? she was asking. I don't think she heard me say there isn't much time left in the day for missing home.

Ruth has been working in the mills for five years. She misses her home and family. She has not been home for a visit all year. She said all this in a dreamy way.

Clarissa Burroughs wets her lips with the tip of her tongue and plays with her long, black hair while she talks. You can tell she thinks she's prettier than she is. Truth is she's harsh-looking. She watched me like a hawk the whole night, didn't take her eyes off me, not even while she was talking to Annie. She's a crooked one, that Clarissa Burroughs. If she swallowed a knitting needle 'twould come out a corkscrew.

Clarissa Burroughs and Annie Clark are as different as night and day. How they can be friends is a mystery to me.

I have never eaten so much food. My plate was bare, but then came dessert: coffee, tea, blueberry pie, and ice cream. To be sure, ice cream is so much better than potatoes. I wanted to take some home to Aunt Nora, 'twas that good.

After dinner the tables were cleared and placed against the walls. Mrs. Jackson brought out a pot of tea and then went into her room.

Ruth went upstairs to write some letters. I stayed and sat with Annie and the other girls.

Laura talked with two girls about a book they were reading while Clarissa boasted about a lecture she had been to. The other girls read or sewed or looked at magazines. 'Twas hard for me to understand what they were talking about. They all have that Lowell way of talking. So fast and so sure. I don't have enough learning to keep up.

Annie wanted to show me her room. Clarissa came with us. I think she just didn't want Annie and me to be alone.

Annie shares her room with Ruth, Laura, and Clarissa. 'Tis filled with beds, trunks, and bandboxes of all shapes and sizes. There is little room to spare. They use the trunks for seats and the bandboxes as writing tables.

The ceiling slopes down so much that we could only stand in the middle of the room.

Clarissa looked at the gold watch she wears and reminded Annie 'twas nearing ten o'clock. The doors have to be locked then because of the curfew. Clarissa said she was sure I didn't want to be stuck there all night.

Just as we reached the front hall, Ruth Shattuck came running down the stairs, calling that she hoped I would visit them again soon. 'Twas nice of her to say so. She reminds me of Maureen. Maureen's dreamy, too.

"Ruth has a pure heart," Annie said when we were outside. "Perhaps too pure."

I was about to be asking what she meant, but she told me to go, 'twas late enough.

The night was as black as can be. I could not see my hand in front of my face. As I came to the Acre I quickened my pace. Lately there has been much strife between neighboring clans. You would think they would have left these feuds back in Ireland. The Irish boys are forever throwing stones at each other over one slight or another. On my way home I spied one of the constables patroling the area. I was fortunate that I did not encounter any difficulty.

I slept little, thinking about my first American friend.

Monday, August 16, 1847
Lowell

Mr. Byrnes was buried today. Aunt Nora said you should never dig a grave on a Monday.

Wednesday, August 18, 1847
Lowell

Lord have mercy. I don't see how we all can fit into the Acre. There are already too many of us, and more Irish arrive every day.

Aunt Nora and I were seeing how our wee

neighbor Fiona Buckley is faring. She was walking home down Dublin Street last night and got caught in the middle of some Irish lads. They hit her in the head with one of their stones, and the poor girl bruised her knees when she ran and fell.

The Buckleys live at the end of a narrow lane, in a tar-paper shack, not a wood house like Aunt Nora's. They don't even have windows to let in the light. There was a piece of horseshoe nailed by the door. Aunt Nora says 'tis to keep bad spirits from entering the house.

Father Callahan was there when we arrived, seeing to the poor girl. She was sleeping soundly, and he said she was more frightened than anything else. I think he said that to quiet Mrs. Buckley. Who can blame her for weeping? Fiona is but a child.

So many people live with Fiona Buckley that there is barely room to stand. Fiona sleeps in a bed with her sister Kathleen and six others. The rest sleep on the floor.

We told Mrs. Buckley that we would be visiting again soon. Mr. Buckley just sat in the corner. He is as odd-looking as two left feet, that one. His black hair is plastered down so it looks like 'twould crack into a thousand pieces if you hit him with a hammer.

I told Aunt Nora that on the way home and we had a good laugh.

Thursday, August 19, 1847
Lowell

Aunt Nora claims to have knowledge of the future. She sees grave events looming on the horizon for me. Soon I will be faced with an important decision. "When the wheel has come full circle," she said.

'Tis putting a fright into me, this kind of talk. She was preparing to tell me more, and I put a stop to it. I have no need to see into the future — the present is quite enough, if you don't mind. I told her I wanted my life to unfold at its own pace.

She smiled and said, "So it will, dearest Mary, so it will."

Sometimes Aunt Nora gives me the chills.

Friday, August 20, 1847
Lowell

I saw Eunice Currier today. She works in the dressing room, where the cloth is finished, and lucky, she is. The air is cleaner, and there is much less noise than in the spinning room. If I could work in the dressing room I would get more pay. But no Irish girls work there. Only Yankee girls.

Annie Clark invited me to visit the shops with her and Laura Austin tomorrow. I could barely stop from throwing my arms around her. Having Annie has made the world seem brighter.

She warned me that she and Laura usually don't buy anything. They just go to look. That suits me fine. Monday is my first payday. And I'm sure I have no money to spare, even if I should be paid at this very instant.

<hr />

'Twas a fine day, the sun shining, the sky blue, and the trees trying to turn red and orange.

The streets of Lowell are clean and made of stone. How different from the Acre, where the streets are quick to turn to mud after a rain.

Merrimack Street is so wide and straight that horses, wagons, and shiny black carriages parade up and down. There are fancy ladies riding in the carriages. They wear wide-brimmed straw bonnets, and their cheeks are painted red.

I asked Laura and Annie why the fancy ladies paint their cheeks, and they both laughed. "To attract their prey," Laura said.

I must have looked puzzled.

"They are looking to snare a man," she said. Annie asked me if I thought they looked pretty. I wasn't sure of the right thing to say. I couldn't tell if they looked pretty or silly. I decided to be silent.

Annie and Laura showed me the library and a grand hotel called the Merrimack House. We went by the depot just in time. A long line of cars was only then pulling in. 'Twas like a giant iron serpent. How that one car pulls all the others is a mystery.

The shops all look new. Their windows show what can be found inside: dresses, shoes, boots, bonnets, combs, shawls, and jewelry. One store has jars of striped candy, chocolate, molasses, raisins, bread, crackers, and barrels of sugar, flour, and rice.

In America there is everything.

My favorite store had a wooden doll, sitting in the window, with bright red lips and yellow hair. For a sad moment I was thinking of the doll Sean got for Molly and Sophie. I wonder where they are. I hope they are safe, like in the dream. I hope Brendan and Sean are safe, too. 'Twould be nice to walk down Merrimack Street with Sean. I wonder if Laura and Annie would like him.

Annie wanted to stop in the bookstore. "Just for a look," she said. Laura tugged at my arm so we could lag behind. She whispered in my ear that Annie won't be able to resist buying a book. 'Tis a quick tongue Laura has and a ready smile to go with it.

'Twas like in a trance Annie was, once we were inside. She walked slowly by the books, as if they were colorful birds and she was choosing one for a pet. Pick one up, she would, read it a bit, and gently put it back down. I saw her draw one close and breathe deeply.

Glad, I was, that Laura Austin wanted to be leaving. I stood the whole time, watching the people passing by the storefront window. I find people so much more interesting than books.

Annie did buy a book. Laura was right.

Sunday, August 22, 1847
Lowell

Kate has come back. She was waiting when we returned from Mass.

On and on she went about Rhode Island. Mrs. Abbott's sister is even richer than Mrs. Abbott. Their house is grander, and they have more servants. Thanks to the beaches and the cool summer breezes they did not suffer because of the heat. Blessed Mother, how relieved I was to hear that.

Kate paints her cheeks now. Just like the ladies in the carriages.

Aunt Nora asked her if she would be staying for supper. I was stirring the stew pot hanging over the fire — there was plenty. But Kate said she wanted to be getting back before dark.

When she left, Aunt Nora said, "Those who travel seldom return holy."

Monday, August 23, 1847
Lowell

My first payday.

'Twas a long time to be waiting. Two weeks before I was put on the payroll. And then pay is once a month.

We lined up as soon as the closing bell rang. The line was so long, I feared they would run out of money by the time they came to me. When I reached the paymaster, he handed me my earnings. At last. How good it felt to hold it in my hands.

I have given the money to Aunt Nora for safekeeping. She put it with the money she is setting aside from her teacher's pay. We counted how much we have. 'Tisn't as much as I'd hoped. 'Twill be a long time before we can send for Ma and Da.

Tuesday, August 24, 1847
Lowell

One of the girls in the weaving room was hurt today. God help her, a shuttle flew off the loom and hit her above the eye. I did not see her, but Laura says she was hurt badly. Knowing how fast those shuttles fly, 'tisn't a surprise to me.

Laura works in the weaving room. She has been here three years. She says that the weaving room is even worse than the spinning room. 'Tis hotter and the noise is greater.

'Tis always hot in the mills. Today two girls fainted before the noon bell. Laura says the corporation doesn't want the thread to become brittle and break. I asked if they worried that we might become brittle and break.

Laura said the corporation won't allow water buckets in the rooms. They think we'll take too much time drinking water. Imagine. I am thirsty all the time now because my throat is so sore. 'Tis hard to breathe, and the lint flies everywhere. I stand on the staircase just to get some air.

My dress always soaks through. So do the other girls'. Some tuck handkerchiefs in their sleeves, but I don't. 'Tisn't a help. They just become soaked, too.

Thursday, August 26, 1847
Lowell

I went to work even though I feel poorly. If I don't work, I don't get paid.

Aunt Nora went to making raspberry leaves steeped in sugar-sweetened water. She gave it to me from her favorite tin cup. I am to gargle every evening for three days and take walks in the countryside after Mass on Sundays. Aunt Nora said she has seen too many girls get sick, working in the mills. Fresh air, "that's the ticket," she says.

Sunday 'tis walking with Annie, I am. I will get some air then.

Aunt Nora made me an onion boiled in milk. 'Twas good, and I am feeling a wee bit better.

I am writing to Mr. Quinn. No letter from him in some time. I want to know how Alice O'Donnell is and how Sean is faring. I wish he were here. Lord knows there is work for him. The Irish lads are building all over Lowell. Working on the new canal, they are. Surely Sean could find work here.

If only Annie and Laura could meet him. They would like each other, now I am sure. They are all so true.

Monday, August 30, 1847
Lowell

Aunt Nora is in great pain. She had to have a tooth out. The top of the tooth came off, wouldn't you know it, while the root remained. It took twenty-five pulls before 'twas over. So weak she was, she could not teach today. Aunt Nora doesn't like to miss school. The children mean the world to her. Her "little scholars," she calls them. Mrs. Buckley watched over her till I returned from the mills. (Mrs. Delaney was here all day, but 'tisn't saying much.) I was glad to hear Fiona is feeling much better, though she is still afraid to walk down Dublin Street alone. And who's to blame her?

My cough continues. I slept little and was tired in the morning.

❈

Tuesday, August 31, 1847
Lowell

Aunt Nora is still in pain, with her cheeks all swollen. I begged her to stay home again today, but she was having none of it. Stubborn as a mule, she is.

Wednesday, September 1, 1847
Lowell

Mrs. Delaney is greatly relieved. A letter from her son came yesterday. She asked me to read it to her. John has found work digging holes in a cemetery. They work all day, and there is little time to rest, but he is thankful not to be working in a factory because one of his chums died from a boiler explosion. The poor boy was scalded so badly, they could not save him.

I didn't read that part to Mrs. Delaney. She'd just go to worrying. I read the rest as he wrote it.

The pay is good — eighty cents a day. He is

saving every penny and hopes to return home by Christmas.

"Sorry to be troubling you," she said. "You're a good lass." She gripped my arm tightly. It felt as if I were being held by the claws of an awful, big bird.

Thursday, September 2, 1847
Lowell

Mr. Fowler dismissed one of the girls. She has not been at work for the past two days. Laura says Mr. Fowler drives us so hard because of the premium the corporation pays him. The more work he gets out of us, the more money he makes.

My head aches terribly, but I am sure to come to the mills just the same. Lord knows I am used to hard work. But doing the same thing over and over is tiring.

Aunt Nora placed a cold cloth on my forehead, which stopped the throbbing, but only for a while.

One of the girls was caught reading her Bible instead of tending her machine. Took the heavy end of the stick, she did. Mr. Fowler was so angry, I thought his eyes would pop right out of his head. He took her Bible and threw it into his desk.

Reading is not allowed in the spinning room. Some of the Yankee girls bring little clippings of poetry and favorite hymns. They paste them on the sides of the window, near the geraniums, and glance at them from time to time.

Mr. Fowler watched me all afternoon. No matter where he was in the room I could feel his eyes following my every move.

Talked about everything under the sun, Annie and me. Having to leave home. Working in the mills. The girls at the boardinghouse.

Annie says she doesn't mind mill work. It lets her lay aside enough money. She wants to work just one more year. Then she'll set off on her own.

She is lucky to be living at the boardinghouse. 'Tis so much nicer than the Acre. Annie said that it is. Mill work has helped her see that there is more to life than working on a farm. And for that she is grateful.

But she does not like having to go to church every Sunday, Mrs. Jackson keeping a sharp eye on their coming and going, and peddlers disturbing them at night, selling their ribbons, shoes, jewelry, and candy.

She can barely find the time to write her poetry. I told her about my diary. 'Twas the first time I ever told anyone. It just jumped out of my mouth. Annie said I never cease to surprise her.

What bothers her most is being with people all day, every day, even when she eats and sleeps.

I thought she liked Laura, Ruth, and Clarissa. I thought they were her friends. Annie said she does like Laura and Ruth. They are like sisters to her — and just as precious. Still, there are times when she wants to be alone.

Seemed to me all the Yankee girls were happy. They are always chirping away like little birds.

"Even the caged bird sings," Annie said, sounding just like Aunt Nora.

As for Clarissa, she said, nothing is worse than listening to her after she returns from one of her lectures. Annie says that Clarissa understands nothing but speaks at great length.

I wish I could be more like Annie. She is so sure of herself. She knows what she thinks and isn't afraid to say it. She says I am shy. I told her that I'm not shy, just quiet. At least I'm not as shy as I was, that's what Aunt Nora says. It seems I'm always talking about Aunt Nora, and now Annie wants to meet her.

I was thinking someone like Annie wouldn't want to come to the Acre. But she just stood there looking at me, so I invited her for a wee visit on Sunday. She said she would be "delighted."

Aunt Nora thinks 'tis a fine idea. "'Twill be nice to have a friend for your birthday," she said.

I had forgotten.
Next Sunday is my birthday.
I will be fifteen.

Monday, September 6, 1847
Lowell

One of the wee boys who cleans the machines got his finger caught today. It was snapped right off. Their hands are small enough to get into the hard-to-reach places, but they are in great danger because of this.

The lad was near me when it happened. As soon as I heard him cry out, I rushed over and picked him up in my arms. Mr. Fowler was there in a flash and grabbed the boy from me. He told me to return at once to my machine. I would have liked to stay with the boy, but Mr. Fowler looked at me with those dull gray eyes of his. He's all eyes and no sight, that one.

I said a prayer for the boy, but there is little I can do that will change anything.

Yesterday I heard Clarissa Burroughs talking about the Irish again. She didn't know I was near. She was talking so loud, 'twas hard not to hear.

She said that the mill agents like the Irish girls because we take all the lower-paying jobs and we have to take what we can get. "Just look where they live — in shantytowns like the Acre. That's where that Mary Driscoll lives." She started imitating how I speak. Everyone laughed. "The Irish should stay in Ireland, where they belong," Clarissa Burroughs said.

The hairs were standing along the back of my neck, and my cheeks were burning like red-hot coals. I went over to where she stood, tapped her on the shoulder, I did. When she turned around 'twas plain I was not who she was expecting to see.

I asked her if she would stay "where she belonged" if there was no food to eat and everyone around her was starving? If leaving was her only hope? "Would you stay, Clarissa?" I said.

She looked at me, her dark eyes blinking. 'Twas like she was trying to make me disappear. Her mouth stayed open, but no sound was I hearing. We were standing so close, I could smell her.

I was after raising my voice, and some of the Yankee girls had gathered around. They were staring and talking to one another and began moving aside to let someone through. 'Twas Annie. Before I knew it, she had joined us in the center of the ring. I have never seen her look that way, like an animal sniffing the air, waiting to be sure before making a move.

She took my arm and pulled me away from Clarissa Burroughs. Then she stepped in between us. She was standing right in front of me, her back to Clarissa. "Pay her no mind," she whispered.

I wanted to tell Annie that I was sorry, but truly I wasn't. Annie didn't give me a chance. She left as suddenly as she had appeared. The other girls stepped aside, letting her pass through the same way she came.

I was once again facing Clarissa. She wasn't blinking anymore, but her mouth was still open.

She came to me, stopping just inches away. "I knew you were trouble the moment I saw you," she said. Her voice was shaking and so was she. "From the moment I saw you."

Then she turned quickly and walked away, making a swooshing sound with her skirt.

I told Aunt Nora everything. She looked sad. "If truth be told," she said, "Clarissa Burroughs is right. We Irish are not where we belong."

'Tis a sorrowful thought.

Wednesday, September 8, 1847
Lowell

I asked Annie why the Yankee girls don't like the Irish.

She said they blame us for what happened at the mills. They say that factory work was better before there were so many Irish. There was time to sit and rest. Now the corporation doesn't care about the girls the way they once did. There are enough Irish girls looking for work that they don't have to.

Why the Irish are to blame for all of this I wasn't understanding. Surely we aren't the reason the windows are nailed shut. Or why the rooms are always hot and so filled with dirt, you can hardly breathe. Is it our fault that the days are long? Wouldn't we prefer a ten-hour day, too?

But I was afraid to say any of that. The words were in my head clear enough, but I wasn't sure they would come out that way. I could feel my heart pounding in my chest.

Still, I decided to ask one question that would not wait.

"What about you? You talk to me, and I'm Irish."

"You're different," Annie said. "You're not like the rest."

Thursday, September 9, 1847
Lowell

Ruth Shattuck is ill with a fever. Annie says that she is delirious and sleeps fitfully. I went back with Annie to the boardinghouse during the noon meal. Ruth was sleeping, so we didn't disturb her. Annie is greatly troubled by her condition.

Friday, September 10, 1847
Lowell

The boy who got his finger snapped off was back in the mills today. When he saw me he came right over and said thank you, very politely. I asked him his name, and he said Sylvester Sawyer. Such a big name for such a wee boy.

Sunday, September 12, 1847
Lowell

At noon a knock was given at the door. We had just come home from Mass. 'Twas Annie, as planned. I was glad that she met with no difficulties.

Aunt Nora made a special birthday dinner. Corned beef, cabbage, and roast potatoes. There was more, too — a cake of fine wheaten bread mixed with honey.

Annie was surprised that I am only fifteen. She said I act older than my age. She said I should have told her 'twas my birthday. Now she wants to be thinking of a present for me. I told her there is no need, which is so.

Once Annie told Aunt Nora that she believes in ghosts there was no stopping them. They had a lively talk about what Annie calls "the spirit world." They agreed that ghosts are poor souls stuck between this life and the next.

The two of them are dear to me, but both live with their heads in the clouds.

After tea Annie asked if we would like to hear one of her poems. I'd never heard one before. She must have approved of Aunt Nora, else she wouldn't have offered, if you ask me.

She reached into her sack and took out her little poetry-writing book. Aunt Nora moved from the table to the rocking chair. Then she said there was nothing she liked more than to hear a fine piece of writing.

Annie read in her soft, soothing voice.

In the poem, a small girl gets lost in a thick forest. Trying to find her way back home, she comes upon a note tacked to a tree. The note invites her to climb to the top. Once there she will be able to see her future.

The tree is the oldest and tallest in the forest. But the branches are low and good for climbing. She climbs the tree to the very top, and when she gets there — just as the note promised — she sees all the days of her life laid out before her. "Like an endless sentence," is the way Annie says it.

Then, when she climbs down from the tree the note is gone. That's the end of the poem.

Annie asked if we liked it. Truth is I wanted to know what the girl saw and what happened to the note. If 'twasn't there when she came down, who took it then? But I held my tongue thinking these were silly questions.

Aunt Nora was wiping tears from her eyes. I didn't think the poem was sad. But I'm not one for poetry.

Annie asked Aunt Nora what she thought.

Aunt Nora said her niece was blessed to have found a friend such as she.

That's the only time I've ever seen Annie blush.

'Tis my first birthday without Ma and Da. We have not heard from them in some time.

Monday, September 13, 1847
Lowell

Everyone is talking about Clarissa Burroughs getting caught.

She was secretly meeting a boy in the mill yard when the night watchman came upon them. They were startled and ran from him. But when they tried to climb over the fence, Clarissa's dress got caught on one of the spikes. The watchman called for help. I understand it took quite a while to get her down.

Annie said Clarissa didn't utter a word to anyone last night and went to bed without eating. In the morning she remained in bed, saying she felt poorly. She is not in work today. Annie said Mrs. Jackson would surely have something to say about this. No one knows what has happened to the boy.

Wednesday, September 15, 1847
Lowell

Each day I am becoming better acquainted with my machines. That's what Annie says. I have nimble fingers and am doing better than she expected in such a short period of time.

Sometimes, however, I still fear I won't be able to do my tasks properly. Thank the Lord that this is only fleeting, and I tend to my machines without mishap.

Thursday, September 16, 1847
Lowell

Ruth is feeling better and is back at work. 'Twas so good to see her. I gave her a big hello, and she smiled.

Sunday, September 19, 1847
Lowell

Aunt Nora was eager to get to church this morning. St. Patrick's has a new organ now. Aunt Nora says the old one was too small.

Later I met Annie, and we talked away the afternoon.

I told her how much I miss Ma and Da. I have not said a word to anyone. Not even Aunt Nora.

Annie told me about her family. 'Tis a sad story.

Annie is the youngest and only girl. She has five brothers. Her mother used to hit her with a small branch she kept hidden in the kitchen. Annie couldn't understand why her mother hated her so.

Then one day she found out from Jed, her oldest brother, that she was not her real mother. Her real mother had died giving birth to her. At first Annie couldn't believe it. But the more she thought about it, the truer it became.

A week after she found out, she left to find work in Lowell. "Lowell was my salvation," she said.

She would like to write Jed but is afraid to let anyone know where she is.

Later, Annie gave me my present. 'Twas in a box all nicely tied up with violet ribbons. Inside was a delicate shawl wrapped around a book of poems. I threw the shawl over my shoulder, and Annie said not to forget about the book.

She is forever reading, and I know she thinks I should. Imagine spending money for a book. She said that 'tis every individual's responsibility to improve their minds. I have to bite my lip to keep from laughing when Annie talks like that. I told her I was more interested in improving my purse than my mind. She laughed and said, "I suppose you are, Mary Driscoll."

Then I hugged her by way of thanks.

Merciful Lord, a letter from Sean.

He is building a road. The bosses treat them like animals, and the people in town do not like them being around. They think there are already too many Irish. And they work cheap, and this makes it bad for everyone.

A boy from County Kerry was killed when a huge rock fell on him. 'Twas being lifted when the chain broke. Another boy was killed by a gunpowder blast. The blast sent rocks flying, and he was struck in the head while taking a drink of water. Bless us and save us, there are so many sad stories like these.

Sean says that Americans do not like the Irish. He's thinking now 'twas a mistake to come here. America is not the way he thought 'twould be. 'Tisn't the way I thought 'twould be, either, but better than back home. At least here there is food to eat and hope for tomorrow.

Sean has visited Alice O'Donnell. The convent is nearby, and he says she is being taken care of.

That puts my mind at ease. 'Twas good of Sean to go see her. He's a dear boy with a good heart. None better.

Mr. Fowler was eyeing me all morning. Buzzing around like a maddened fly, he was.

In the afternoon he crept up on me, silent as a mouse. I did not see him until he was right on me. I could feel his breath on my neck.

"Don't let your mind wander, Mary", he hissed into my ear. 'Twas a miracle I could hear him above the noise, but he was standing very, very close. I was as scared as a rabbit in its burrow.

Annie showed me the signal they use to warn each other that Mr. Fowler is coming. 'Tis making a circle with your arms over your head. I have always wondered why they do that. He won't catch me again.

Friday, September 24, 1847
Lowell

Ruth Shattuck walked out today. Some of her bobbins began falling on the floor, making quite a clatter. She just stood there looking at them with that dreamy look in her eyes. Watched them fall like they weren't even hers. Then she ran out of the spinning room without an if-you-don't-mind to anyone.

I went back with Annie just as soon as the seven o'clock bell rang. Ruth was packing when we arrived.

Annie tried to convince her to stay, but she wasn't hearing any of it. Talking away, she was, while she packed. Annie and I sat on the bed and listened. 'Twas all we could do.

"I don't have eyes in the back of my head. I can't tend that many machines without going mad. I need fresh air. I am going home where there are no bells, bells, bells. Bells that tell you when you can open your eyes and when you can close them. When you can sleep and when you can eat.

I don't know if I'll ever get those bells out of my head."

Thanks be to the Lord, Annie was able to get her to wait till tomorrow. Then Annie will take her to the stagecoach.

I have never seen Annie this upset. Usually she runs as deep as the ocean.

Downstairs, as I was leaving, she said 'twas a shame, and Ruth is a fine girl. She is that.

On the way home, I thought about the look in Ruth's eyes. "I have been here too long," she said. I hope I'm not here too long.

Monday, September 27, 1847
Lowell

Another payday. Aunt Nora and I counted the money we have. Like a hive hoards honey, we lay away money for Ma and Da.

Clarissa Burrough's beautiful long, black hair was caught in her machine, and her scalp was pulled off. Glory of God, 'twas a frightful spectacle.

Her howls of pain were loud enough to be heard above the roar of the machines. It took forever to stop them. By the time Mr. Fowler cut off her hair and pulled her away, 'twas too late.

There was utter silence.

Mr. Fowler wasted no time. He was more concerned that the machines were down than the fate of the girl. As soon as her limp body was removed from the room, he pulled the cord and ordered everyone back to work.

Ruth had warned Clarissa not to wear her hair that way. She showed her how to fix it up so 'twouldn't get caught, because this has happened before. Ruth warned her how dangerous 'twas, but Clarissa would not listen. She insisted on leaving her hair loose because she was so proud of how long and shiny 'twas. But look where her pride has gotten her now.

I have not slept since this happened.

Kate came by for a chat.

Bless the day, she only stayed a wee minute. She was finding out if Aunt Nora knew any love potions. Wouldn't you know she did. Much good, Aunt Nora said, could come from sprinkling water that has washed a child's feet outside your door.

'Twas just what Kate was after. Having what she came for, she got up to leave. Aunt Nora asked her if she is planning to marry. Kate said she might be and left as suddenly as she came.

I told Annie about Kate and the love potions.

Annie asked if I wanted to marry. "I am too young," I told her.

"When you are old enough. Would you choose to then?"

"Marriage is fine if you're rich, like Mrs. Abbott. If you're not rich what do you have to look forward to? Hoping your husband will provide? 'Tisn't enough for me," I told her.

Annie said 'twould be a shame if a pretty girl like me never marries.

When I asked if Annie would marry, she said she is a restless spirit.

She would like to be on her own for a while. To live where she wants and go where she pleases. She doesn't think you can do that if you're married.

"But then," she said, "when I've had my fill, I'll find my true love and live happily ever after." It sounded like one of those books Annie gets from the library.

"And what will your true love be like, dear Annie?" I asked.

She grabbed my shoulders with both her hands and said, "Why, just like Mr. Fowler, of course."

We went to laughing so hard that we fell down on top of each other and rolled in the freshly fallen snow.

Tuesday, October 5, 1847
Lowell

Laura Austin fears her name is on the list because she was handing out a labor newspaper. There is a list of girls who the corporation thinks are troublemakers. If you are dismissed, they send the list to the other mills in the area. That way you can't find work and cause more trouble.

Laura was one of the girls in the turnout last year when they were striking for a ten-hour day. They got more time for their meals but 'twas all. Laura said they all signed the petition, but it came to nothing. "The corporation won," Laura said, "just like it always does."

When Laura first came to Lowell — six years ago — the girls stood by one another. Then, she said, no girl tended more than two looms. There was time to sit and rest. Now, she says, some girls tend four or five machines. The corporations speed up the machines and slow down the clocks so we work longer and get paid less.

'Twould be nice to work only ten hours. I can only imagine.

Still, if truth be told, I am glad not to have to sign anything. For myself, I would sign. I have nothing to fear. But I have Ma and Da to think about.

When I have enough money for their passage, when they are here beside me, then I can think of such things, but not now. That is not what I came to America for.

Friday, October 8, 1847
Lowell

Ma and Da will not be coming.

Something was terribly wrong, I just knew it. Aunt Nora is always so cheerful — humming a tune more likely than not. But she was sitting at the table, quiet, resting her head in one hand and holding a letter in the other. When she looked up, I could see that she had been crying. 'Twas like the light had left her eyes.

She didn't want me to read the letter. She said there was no need. 'Twas from Father Mullaney. He said little. Only what was needed. That they are gone.

I feel lost. I should never have left Ireland. Never.

Saturday, October 9, 1847
Lowell

Mrs. Buckley and Fiona visited. Later Annie came. 'Twas kind of her. She brought me chocolate and raisins. She worried when I wasn't in the mills. And then, last night, Aunt Nora went to Mrs. Jackson's to tell her. Dear Aunt Nora. Now she has gone to talk to Kate.

Sunday, October 10, 1847
Lowell

Annie and Laura came. They are so dear to take the time.

My cough has worsened, but 'tis best I return to work on Monday. There is nothing for me to do here. Staying in bed does no good. I think too much about Ma and Da.

Last night Aunt Nora held me and rocked me back and forth, singing Ma's lullaby:

> *On the wings of the wind*
> *Over the dark rolling deep*
> *Angels are coming*
> *To watch over thy sleep*
>
> *Angels are coming*
> *To watch over thee*
> *So list' to the wind*
> *Coming over the sea*

Writing down the words helps to calm me, for I can hear Ma's voice when I see the words on the page.

If only Ma could hold me one last time.

I cried so long and so hard that I cried myself to sleep.

Monday, October 11, 1847
Lowell

I do my work. It helps me pass the time. Knowing Annie is near also helps.

Thursday, October 14, 1847
Lowell

I look out the mill windows and wonder just how far Ireland is from where I am. It seems 'twas only yesterday Ma said I would be going to America. Now it feels like so very long ago, beyond my memory's reach. Like 'twasn't even me.

If Mrs. Delaney doesn't stop staring at me soon I'll go mad. John is returning next week.

Friday, October 15, 1847
Lowell

Laura Austin said her name is on the list. One of the girls saw it. There is a check next to her name and then it says, "willful."

Monday, October 18, 1847
Lowell

The oil lamps were lit this morning and again this evening so that we could work in the dark. Many of the girls complain. They don't like the foul smell, and they don't like being forced to work by lamplight.

Wednesday, October 20, 1847
Lowell

I am worn. Standing all day has caused my feet to ache terribly. Nothing relieves the pain. Weariness has crept into my bones. My eyes feel as if they will burst from my head thanks to the endless noise. The lint flies everywhere. Breathing itself is a burden.

At night my chest heaves painfully. I wake as tired as when I lay down.

Thursday, October 28, 1847
Lowell

The trees are bare and covered with last night's snowfall. 'Tis windy and icy. I walk carefully so as not to fall.

Aunt Nora stuffed paper into the toes of my boots to help keep me warm. She reminded me to leave them in front of the fireplace when they are wet so they will be dry in the morning.

'Tis a chill I caught going from the hot spinning room into the cold night air. Aunt Nora rubbed my hands before we went to sleep. "God save the poor," she said when she was done.

'Tis dark in the morning when I leave and dark when I return. I hardly see the sun. It makes me gloomy.

Monday, November 1, 1847
Lowell

I stirred the fire carefully before I slept. I was feeling poorly last night. My cough disturbs my sleep. When I awoke the fire had gone out. Aunt Nora had to send John Delaney to Mrs. Buckley's for some live coals.

Saturday, November 6, 1847
Lowell

I have read Mr. Quinn's letter over and over. I am pasting it here so I will never forget it.

Dear Mary Driscoll,

'Tis my unpleasant task to inform you of the sorrowful events that have recently taken place.

There has been much tension in the air. The Yankees seem to dislike we Irish more with each passing week.

On Monday past, a mob, angered by ru-

mors that Irish lads had treated an American flag rudely, formed in the streets of Arlington. Arlington, as you know, is the location of the convent to which Alice O'Donnell has been entrusted.

By nightfall the unruly mob was headed for the Irish district. They attacked homes and churches, destroying everything in their path. Many on both sides were bleeding and wounded. The melee continued for two days and two nights and grew more deadly with each passing hour. As darkness fell on the second night, the mob, having no regard for either man or God, made for the convent.

During the two days of rioting, word spread to nearby Somerville, where my nephew Sean was working. Fearing for Alice O'Donnell's safety, he made his way to Arlington. There he joined with others who were working to restore order. He helped evacuate the convent and saw to it that Alice was in safe hands.

He then returned to the convent. The mob

had set fire to the now-empty building, which was soon engulfed in flames.

Although, thank the Lord, none of the children were hurt, Sean and three other Irish lads have been charged as accessories to murder because two of the Yankees died from head wounds received during the rock-throwing riot.

Sean protested that he was not in Arlington at the time of the violence — he was still in Somerville — but his words fell on deaf ears as you might imagine.

I am presently occupied with trying to raise the bail money necessary to free Sean from his jail cell, where he awaits trial. The amount is quite steep, and although I am, of course, taking all necessary steps, I cannot say that I am hopeful. I am proceeding as quickly as possible for there is grave talk here that the boys will not be allowed to live long enough to stand trial.

Alice is with us now. She is sleeping near me as I write. She will, of course, remain here *as long as necessary, so have no fear in that regard.*

What the result of all this will be only heaven knows. The Lord will, I am certain, reward the good and condemn the evil to unceasing flames.

Respectfully,
Patrick Quinn

I ran all the way to Annie's. 'Twas cold and the snow was blowing in my face, making it hard to breathe. I hadn't given a moment's thought to what I would do if Annie wasn't there. Thankfully she was. Mrs. Jackson let me go right up.

Annie was writing in one of her books and Laura lay beside her, chatting away. I was glad, too, that Laura was there. They saw on my face that something was terribly wrong and Laura made room for me on the wee bed. I told them all that Mr. Quinn had written and my plan.

Laura said nothing, but Annie said right out she wouldn't let me go. I had to think of myself first, she said. Not Sean or Alice O'Donnell. She said she is sure Mr. Quinn will see to Alice's safety.

Maybe so. Maybe not.

And what of Sean? I asked her. What would I do, just let him sit in jail? Wait till Mr. Quinn writes me again, this time to tell me how the Yankees dragged him into the street and beat him to death just because he is Irish?

I cannot see with anyone's eyes but my own. I must go to Boston. I must take the money I put aside for Ma and Da and bring it to Sean.

Suddenly Laura broke her silence. "I'll go with you," she said. I could hardly believe my ears. "'Tis just a matter of time before I am dismissed, and I have always wanted to see Boston. And now," she said, "I will."

Annie looked shaken by this turn. She asked me if I had told Aunt Nora. I think she hoped Aunt Nora would be able to stop me. I haven't told her because truth be told, I am afraid she will not approve. But I am going whether she approves or not.

I told Aunt Nora I would only take my pay, but she said to take it all. With the Delaneys' board and her own wages, she will have enough.

She hugged me, and then Annie and Laura started to cry. 'Twas a sight. Annie said we'd best be leaving for the depot.

They waited outside while I said one more good-bye to Aunt Nora.

"Quiet One," she said. "Always remember one thing. The Lord would never close one gate without opening another."

The same as Ma said when I left home to come to America. 'Tis true, I hope.

Epilogue

Nora Kinsella, Mary's aunt, continued to teach school in Lowell for thirty-two more years.

Kate Driscoll worked for Mrs. Abbott until 1851 when she met and married Dennis Kelly. They had two children.

Sean Riordan fled Boston as soon as Mary provided the necessary bail money. His whereabouts after 1847 are unknown.

Annie Clark left the mills in 1848, as planned. She traveled west, stopping in Racine, Wisconsin. There she married Silas Marks, one of the town's leading lawyers. She and her husband had no children.

Patrick Quinn's tavern grew in size, doubling as a grocery store by day. He became a wealthy man of property. Although he never ran for elective office, he was so influential in Boston politics that it was said, "You can't win without Quinn." He was loved and respected throughout the Boston Irish community.

Laura Austin and Mary Driscoll, with Quinn's help, placed Alice O'Donnell in the capable hands of the Perkins Institute for the Blind. There Alice learned the manual alphabet and other ways of improving her communication with the outside world. She was well cared for.

Mary Driscoll died in the cholera epidemic of 1849.

She was seventeen.

Life in America
in 1847

Historical Note

Beginning in 1845, Ireland experienced an extended crop failure that became known as the Great Famine. Over the next five years, one million of Ireland's nine million citizens died, and almost two million emigrated to other countries.

The Great Famine was the result of two terrible forces. First, potatoes, the basic crop of Irish tenant farmers, were attacked by a "blight" or fungus. Because the Irish farmers were unable to plant new healthy potato crops, their primary diet, there was widespread starvation. Second, Ireland, subject to British rule since the beginning of the nineteenth century, consisted of large estates owned and managed by English landlords. These estates were divided into small farms, rented at high rates to poor Irish farmers. When half the oat crop failed, farmers were unable to pay their rents, and many landlords evicted them.

Initially, there was little help from the British government. Their "laissez-faire," or "hands-off" approach allowed the large land owners to run their own affairs. As starvation and evictions worsened, the British prime minister, Sir Robert Peel, set up public works programs. Irish men were hired as laborers on make-work construction projects such as "famine roads," which were created more to keep the men busy than to build functioning roads. The wages were very low, not nearly enough to prevent starvation or evictions. What Ireland needed was food and a new farming system.

By 1847, conditions in Ireland had reached catastrophic levels. Many people were reduced to eating seaweed and cabbage leaves, even grass and tree bark. Women with children often left their husbands to move into poorhouses or workhouses for the homeless. Diseases such as typhus, relapsing fever, and dropsy were rampant, bringing death. Public works programs were stopped, and soup kitchens were set up to feed the starving. Each person was allowed to receive two meals of free soup a week. Help came from churches and governments around the world, and the United States Congress authorized millions of dollars for famine relief. These efforts eventually ended the Great Famine, but for many it was too little too late.

The town of Skibbereen in County Cork was the hardest hit in all of Ireland, and the area was known as "the fatal district." So many people died that there weren't enough coffins in which to bury the dead. For the people of Skibbereen and many other parts of Ireland, the only choice was to leave their country. By the early 1850s, approximately one quarter of Ireland's population had left.

The British government encouraged emigration of the Irish to other countries as the solution to their "troublesome problem." Ticket prices for ship passage were kept low. In some cases, English landlords purchased tickets for their tenant farmers, grateful to get rid of them. For most immigrants, however, tickets were bought with money raised by selling their few remaining belongings or with money sent to them by relatives in other countries. A popular saying was, "The only place in Ireland a man can make his fortune is in America."

The voyage to America took at least six weeks, and sometimes more than three months. The cheapest passage was in old wooden slave ships, called "coffin ships," or in steerage on sailing sloops. Passengers were crowded into tiny closed living quarters with little ventilation. Food and water on these ships were scarce. Water was stored in barrels that had formerly carried products like vinegar and turpentine, making it unfit for drinking. On long voyages, meat became tainted, and bread and flour crawled with insects and vermin. Cattle and pigs were treated better than the passengers. Fire was a constant danger, and cooking and smoking were extremely risky. There were few facilities for washing, and because the steerage was so filthy, diseases spread rapidly. In 1847, the worst year of the Great Famine, 7,000 immigrants perished aboard ships, and another 10,000 died after landing in America.

Upon arriving in the United States, immigrants underwent a medical examination. Those who were sick and did not pass the examination were either placed in quarantine until they were well or turned away. Those turned away frequently sailed on to Canada.

In the large port cities of Philadelphia, New York, and Boston, the new immigrants, with high hopes, little money, and few skills, were easily victimized. Their Catholic religion was feared and often scorned, and they faced harsh discrimination and prejudice. When seeking work, they were often rejected by "NINA" signs, which meant "No Irish Need Apply."

In the 1820s, the Industrial Revolution began in Lowell, Massachusetts at the Pawtucket Falls on the Merrimack River. It was a factory in the wilderness, started by young adventuresome investors from well-to-do Boston families. They brought together a new system of textile manufacturing using power looms, a primarily female workforce, and venture capital in order to make money. They were extraordinarily successful.

By 1847, Lowell, a city of 30,000 people, was the center for textile manufacturing in the United States. The Lowell textile mills employed 15,000 workers, two-thirds of whom were young women, between the ages of fifteen and thirty, from New England. Work in the mills was hard, but provided young women with one of the few chances to earn cash wages. To recruit young women to work in the textile mills, the corporations built large, well-run, brick boardinghouses. They encouraged the establishment of churches, and sponsored schools, libraries, hospitals, health clinics, charitable organizations, reading rooms, and lectures. The lectures included popular writers, educators, and activists such as Ralph Waldo Emerson. In the evenings and on weekends, "improvement circles" were held in churches and reading rooms, and young women were encouraged to write poetry and short stories.

These young female workers had a strong sense of independence. They fought for better working conditions, a ten-hour workday, and higher wages. Although not always successful, they used petitions, legislative hearings, walkouts, newspaper editorials, and journal articles to fight for their rights. They published a prolabor newspaper, the *Voice of Industry*, and a literary magazine, *The Lowell Offering*.

When the textile corporations entered upon a major expansion program, they needed additional workers to meet their ambitious plans. The enormous numbers of unskilled famine Irish immigrants who were pouring into America, desperate for jobs, became that new source.

The Lowell factory system began to change in the 1850s. New advanced technology enabled less skilled workers to produce more cloth at lower wages. The directors of the corporations were more interested in profit than in the workers' welfare. Life in the mills became less desirable for the Yankee girls, and mill management shifted recruiting efforts toward immigrants. The poor, uneducated, and unskilled famine Irish had little choice but to endure these hardships in order to survive in their new homeland.

From the founding of Lowell, small numbers of Irish immigrants had come to help construct the power canals and brick mills and boardinghouses. They had established two Catholic churches, opened shops and businesses, and attended city Irish schools taught by Irish women and men. In some ways, these early Irish immigrants paved the way for the famine Irish who followed.

Thousands of Irish immigrants flowed into the United States, surviving and overcoming terrible conditions. Unskilled jobs with low wages required entire families — mothers, fathers, and older children — to work in order to earn a living wage. Discrimination forced families to live in deplorable housing in overcrowded neighborhoods. Religious prejudice and language (many Irish immigrants spoke the Irish language) often isolated and segregated the Irish community. But ultimately, with citizenship and the vote, the Irish gained the opportunity to participate as equals in the American system. Still, even 150 years later, it would be hard to find people of Irish extraction who don't remember the famine and the many hardships their ancestors endured on the way to becoming full-fledged American citizens.

The potato, a cheap but nutritious food, was the principal diet of the poor in Ireland until 1845, when a fungus destroyed most of the crop. The failure of the potato crop was the cause of the Great Famine, in which almost a million Irish people starved to death.

Desperate for basic survival, nearly two million Irish fled their homeland, and half of them came to America. Passage cost little, but the wooden ships were terribly uncomfortable, grossly unsanitary, and easily caught fire. Tens of thousands died at sea.

Lowell, Massachusetts, was the center of textile manufacturing in the 1840s. As workers in the mill, young single women were taught skills of the trade, as well as reading and writing.

One of the most important inventions of the Industrial Revolution was the power loom, which enabled one person to supervise several mechanized looms at once. With fewer workers, textile mills were able to churn out bolts of fabric more quickly. This had an obvious result: profit.

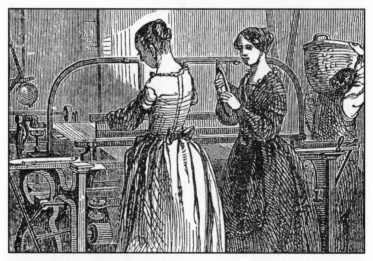

Mill owners, motivated by profit and greed, showed little concern for their workers' welfare. Labor newspapers, such as the Voice of Industry, provided workers with a forum for speaking out against inhumane working conditions.

The "mill girls" wore simple dresses. They kept their long hair pinned up, in order to avoid the dangerous possiblity of getting it caught in the machines.

There was a hierarchy of workers in the mill, according to their skills—from the lowest bobbin girl, who replaced the empty spools, to the weavers, whose skill and practiced eye created the patterns of fabrics. In between, there were spinners, who spun yarn, and drawing-in girls, who threaded yarn for the weavers.

Merrimack was one of the many internationally-known manufacturers of textiles in Lowell, Massachusetts, during this period of time. Cloth fabrics from Lowell were sold and shipped to all parts of the world from nearby ports.

TIME TABLE OF THE LOWELL MILLS,

To take effect on and after Oct. 21st, 1851.

The Standard time being that of the meridian of Lowell, as shown by the regulator clock of JOSEPH RAYNES, 43 Central Street.

	From 1st to 10th inclusive.				From 11th to 20th inclusive.				From 21st to last day of month.			
	1stBell	2dBell	3dBell	Eve.Bell	1stBell	2d Bell	3d Bell	Eve.Bell	1stBell	2dBell	3dBell	Eve.Bell
January,	5.00	6.00	6.50	*7.30	5.00	6 00	6.50	*7.30	5.00	6.00	6.50	*7.30
February,	4.30	5.30	6.40	*7.30	4.30	5.30	6.25	*7.30	4.30	5.30	6.15	*7.30
March,	5.40	6.00		*7.30	5.20	5.40		*7.30	5.05	5.25		6.35
April,	4.45	5.05		6.45	4.30	4.50		6.55	4.30	4.50		7.00
May,	4 30	4.50		7·00	4.30	4.50		7.00	4.30	4.50		7 00
June,	"	"		"	"	"		"	"	"		"
July,	"	"		"	"	"		"	"	"		"
August,	"	"		"	"	"		"	"	"		"
September,	4.40	5.00		6.45	4.50	5.10		6.30	5.00	5.20		*7.30
October,	5.10	5.30		*7.30	5.20	5.40		*7.30	5.35	5.55		*7.30
November,	4.30	5.30	6.10	*7.30	4.30	5.30	6.20	*7.30	5.00	6.00	6.35	*7.30
December,	5.00	6.00	6.45	*7.30	5.00	6.00	6.50	*7.30	5.00	6·00	6.50	*7.30

* Excepting on Saturdays from Sept. 21st to March 20th inclusive, when it is rung at 20 minutes after sunset.

YARD GATES,

Will be opened at ringing of last morning bell, of meal bells, and of evening bells; and kept open Ten minutes.

MILL GATES.

Commence hoisting Mill Gates, Two minutes before commencing work.

WORK COMMENCES,

At Ten minutes after last morning bell, and at Ten minutes after bell which "rings in" from Meals.

BREAKFAST BELLS.

During March "Ring out".........at....7.30 a. m.........."Ring in" at 8.05 a. m.
April 1st to Sept. 20th inclusive....at....7 00 " " .... " " at 7.35 " "
Sept. 21st to Oct. 31st inclusive.....at....7.30 " " .... " " at 8.05 " "
Remainder of year work commences after Breakfast.

DINNER BELLS.

"Ring out".......... ....12.30 p. m........."Ring in".... 1.05 p. m.

In all cases, the *first* stroke of the bell is considered as marking the time.

A worker's life was strictly regulated by the clock. Bells were rung to designate each change of activity and workers were fined for lateness.

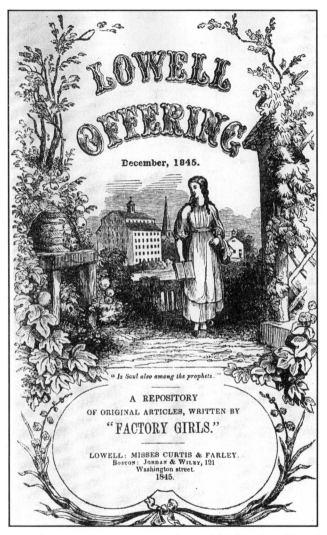

LOWELL OFFERING

December, 1845.

" *Is Saul also among the prophets.* "

A REPOSITORY
OF ORIGINAL ARTICLES, WRITTEN BY
"FACTORY GIRLS."

LOWELL: MISSES CURTIS & FARLEY.
BOSTON: JORDAN & WILEY, 121
Washington street.
1845.

This popular magazine was written by and for female mill workers.
It became an outlet for creative expression, and featured poetry, short
stories, essays, announcements of cultural activities, and advertisements.

159

The town of Lowell was the hub of social activity and a cultural center. The "mill girls" enjoyed a certain independence and could use their wages as they pleased. They went downtown to buy clothes and books; to attend theater, concerts, and poetry readings; and to have tea after church.

St. Patrick's Church became the center of the Irish immigrant social world as well as their religious sanctuary.

Mill agents provided clean, supervised, pleasant boarding houses where the "mill girls" ate together, shared rooms, and had curfews, almost as if they were living in college sororities.

The famine Irish lived mainly in impoverished neighborhoods like the Acre, shown here. Though the photos on this page were not taken until the 1930s, the buildings remain much the same as they were in 1847.

HEAR THE WIND BLOW

Music has always been an important part of Irish culture, and many popular American folk songs have their roots in Ireland. This is one of many songs the Irish brought to the United States, and it was sung wherever they settled from Massachusetts to California.

HEAR THE WIND BLOW
(continued)

1. On the wings of the wind
   Over the dark rolling deep
   Angels are coming
   To watch over thy sleep

   Angels are coming
   To watch over thee
   So list' to the wind
   Coming over the sea

   Hear the wind blow
   Hear the wind blow
   Lean your head over
   Hear the wind blow

2. On wings of the night
   May your fury be crossed
   May no one that's dear
   To our island be lost

   Blow the winds gently
   Calm be the foam
   Shine the light brightly
   To guide them back home

3. The curraghs are sailing
   Way out in the blue
   Laden with herring
   Of silvery hue

   Silver the herring
   Silver the sea
   Soon there'll be silver
   For baby and me

   Hear the wind blow
   Hear the wind blow
   Lean your head over
   Hear the wind blow

4. The curraghs tomorrow
   Will stand on the shore
   And he'll go sailing
   And sailing no more

   The nets will be drying
   Nets haven't passed
   Contented he'll rest
   Safe in my arms

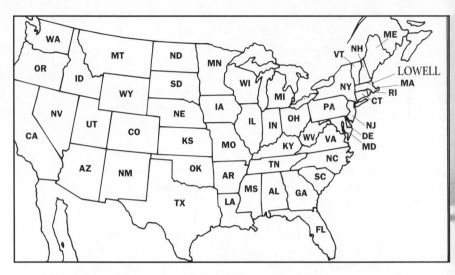

Modern map of the continental United States, showing the approximate location of Lowell, Massachusetts.

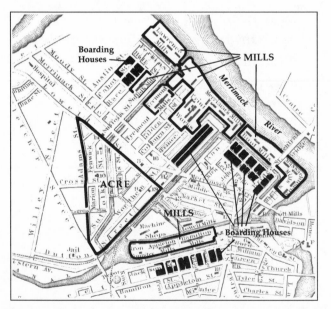

This map shows the main streets of Lowell as they were in 1847.

0

About the Author

Barry Denenberg is the author of several critically acclaimed books for middle-grade and young-adult readers, including one other book in the Dear America series, *When Will This Cruel War Be Over?: The Civil War Diary of Emma Simpson,* which was named an NCSS Notable Children's Trade Book in the Field of Social Studies. Widely praised for his rigorous research, he has written about many important areas of American history, from the Civil War to Vietnam.

"*So Far from Home* illuminates three critical and fascinating aspects of American history," he says. "First, the Lowell mills marked the beginning of the Industrial Revolution in America. Second, the girls who came to work in those mills earned and saved their own money and went on to help shape American society. Lastly, Mary Driscoll can tell us what it was like to be forced to leave the country of your birth and come to the United States with no money, little or no knowledge of the language, few friends, and fewer prospects for earning a living.

"For four hundred years, America has been the land of hope for an incredibly diverse group of immigrants. It is, I think, what makes us unique."

Denenberg's works of nonfiction include, *An American Hero: The True Story of Charles A. Lindbergh*, an ALA Best Book for Young Adults and a New York Public Library Book for the Teenage; and *Voices from Vietnam*, an ALA Best Book for Young Adults, a *Booklist* Editor's Choice Book, and a New York Public Library Book for the Teenage. He lives with his wife and their daughter, Emma, in Westchester County, New York.

*To the memory of
my grandfather, Louis Denenberg*

Acknowledgments

The author would like to thank Martha Mayo at the Center for Lowell History for graciously sharing her intelligence and time.

Grateful acknowledgment is made for permission to reprint the following.

Cover portrait: *Gulnihal* by Frederic Lord Leighton. Exhibited 1886. Oil on canvas. Collection of Andrew Lloyd Webber, Switzerland, by courtesy of Julian Hartnoll.
Cover background: *The Dinner Hour, Wigan* by Eyre Crow. Manchester Museum of Art. Used by permission of Bridgeman/Art Resource, New York.

Page 153: Famine drawing, Library of Congress
Page 154: Passenger ship en route to America, *Harpers Weekly*
Page 155 (top): Merrimack Mills and boarding house, American Textile Museum, Lowell, Massachusetts
Page 155 (bottom): Power loom, ibid.
Page 156 (top): *Voice of Industry,* Lowell Historical Society, Lowell, Massachusetts
Page 156 (bottom): Mill girls at loom, American Textile Museum, Lowell, Massachusetts

Other books in the *Dear America* series

A Journey to the New World
The Diary of Remember Patience Whipple
by Kathryn Lasky

The Winter of Red Snow
The Revolutionary War Diary of Abigail Jane Stewart
by Kristiana Gregory

When Will This Cruel War Be Over?
The Civil War Diary of Emma Simpson
by Barry Denenberg

A Picture of Freedom
The Diary of Clotee, a Slave Girl
by Patricia C. McKissack

Across the Wide and Lonesome Prairie
The Oregon Trail Diary of Hattie Campbell
by Kristiana Gregory

I Thought My Soul Would Rise and Fly
The Diary of Patsy, a Freed Girl
by Joyce Hansen

While the events described and some of the characters
in this book may be based on actual historical events
and real people, Mary Driscoll is a fictional character,
created by the author, and her diary is a work of fiction.

Library of Congress Cataloging-in-Publication Data
Denenberg, Barry.
So far from home : the diary of Mary Driscoll, an Irish mill girl
by Barry Denenberg
p. cm. — (Dear America : 7)
Summary: In the diary account of her journey from Ireland in 1847
and of her work in a mill in Lowell, Massachusetts, fourteen-year-old
Mary reveals a great longing for her family.
ISBN 0-590-92667-5 (alk. paper)
[1. Irish Americans. — Fiction.   2. Immigrants — Fiction.   3. Textile
workers — Fiction.   4. Lowell (Mass.) — Fiction.   5. Diaries — Fiction.]
I. Title   II. Series.
PZ7.D4135So   1997
[Fic] — dc21   97-5846
CIP
AC
12 11 10 9 8 7 6 5 4 3   7 8 9/9 0/0 01 02 03

The display type was set in Tiranti Solid.
The text type was set in Berling.
Book design by Elizabeth B. Parisi

Printed in the U.S.A.   37
First edition, October 1997